GLO
PUB1

Creepy
Tales of the
1910s

Including *Casting the Runes,*
Dracula's Guest, and
The Haunted Pampero

…He switched on another slide, which showed a great mass of snakes, centipedes, and disgusting creatures with wings, and somehow or other he made it seem as if they were climbing out of the picture and getting in amongst the audience…

Creepy Tales of the 1910s

Edited and introduced by
D. EDWARD WRIGHT

Illustrations by
C. RAYMOND HALL

GLOWBUG PUBLISHING

Introduction copyright © Duncan Wright, 2024
Illustrations copyright © C. Raymond Hall, 2024

First published in 2024 by Glowbug Publishing.

Contact us at glowbugpublishing@gmail.com

Browse other Glowbug publications at
www.glowbugpublishing.com

ISBN: 978-1-3999-6790-7

Dates attributed to each story relate to first publication.

A Charming Font by GemFonts / Typotheticals.

Typeset by Glowbug Publishing.

Printed and bound in Great Britain by Imprint Digital.

Table of Contents

Illustrations

Chronicles

Introduction

The legacy of the 1910s lies forever under the shadow of the First World War, a conflict unlike any before in terms of both its geographical reach and degree of mechanised mass murder. While wars had spanned continents before[1] and the Russo-Japanese War of 1904–1905 had already demonstrated the bloody potential of modern warfare, the Great War surpassed these to become one of the deadliest conflicts in history. The decade was also a time of considerable geopolitical change, and bore witness to the fall of empires, birth of nations, and spread of women's suffrage.

Horror stories reflect the fears of the day, and in this decade of total war, the classic ghost stories of the Victorian and Edwardian eras became increasingly quaint, a childish fear of the dark. The ghost story can never be truly exorcised, however, and in the 20th century it began to take on more sinister undertones, as exemplified by the work of M.R. James and E.F. Benson. By the middle of the decade, the Great War started to leave an indelible mark on literature, with not even the ghost story escaping its touch. This influence is epitomised by *The Bowmen* (1914), Arthur Machen's short story about spectral figures coming to the aid of beleaguered British troops, which (much to Machen's dismay) inspired legends of angelic intervention at the Battle of Mons. Following up on the success of *The Bowmen*, Machen wrote a handful of other ghostly war stories, primarily morale-boosting propaganda in which brave British soldiers receive their eternal reward (*The Soldiers' Rest*, 1914) or divine retribution is visited upon histrionically and irredeemably evil Germans (*The Monstrance*, 1915).

---

1   Including the Nine Years' War (1688–1697), the Seven Years' War (1756–1763), and the Napoleonic Wars (1803–1815).

The 1910s were also characterised by the steady rise of "weird fiction," a genre that combines elements of horror, fantasy, and science fiction to create a world imbued with dark, mysterious forces beyond the ken of men. Weird fiction was first defined by H.P. Lovecraft, who while far from the first to pen a story we might consider to be "weird,"[2] produced a body of work that is closely associated with the genre today. Lovecraft made his literary debut in this decade, with his first published story, *The Alchemist*, appearing in the November 1916 issue of *The United Amateur*. He was not the only author of weird fiction to be active at this time; others included Francis Stevens (a pseudonym of Gertrude Barrows Bennett) and William Hope Hodgson, both of whom are represented here. The latter author died at the Fourth Battle of Ypres in 1918, a victim of the horrendous global conflict that claimed over nine million lives.

This anthology collects ten short horror stories, with each tale originally published in a different year of the 1910s.[3] The first two stories (1911–1912) are connected by ideas of fate, premonition, and the evil that lurks in the hearts of men and women. Four of the stories (from 1913, 1917, and 1919–1920) are concerned with the wrath of the natural world, red in tooth, claw, and tentacle. The final four stories (from 1914–1916 and 1918) explore our own bestial side, featuring outsiders suspected of transforming into animals hauntingly familiar…or disturbingly exotic.

---

2   That honour may arguably belong to Edgar Allan Poe (1809–1849) or Nathaniel Hawthorne (1804–1864), if not an earlier writer.

3   Decades start with a year ending in 1 for the simple reason that there was no year 0.

No Fate but What You Make?

The decade in horror was ushered in by the publication of *More Ghost Stories of an Antiquary* by King's College scholar Montague Rhodes James (1862–1936). In the preface of his 1911 collection, James expounded on his formula for writing an effective ghost story, the elements described now considered de rigueur for tales in the "Jamesian" style. Such ghost stories are characterised by the inclusion of a naïve and nondescript gentleman protagonist, an environment and time familiar to the target audience (no more windswept castles in the 14th century), and a slow and steady transition from the safe and commonplace to the perilous and supernatural—all of which were intended to give the target reader the sense that, "*If I'm not very careful, something of this kind may happen to me!*"

A second, contemporaneous writer of ghost stories in the Jamesian style was Edward Frederic Benson MBE (1867–1940). Benson was also an alumnus of King's College, Cambridge, and attended at least one reading of James's ghost stories during his time as an undergraduate.[4] Much like James, Benson updated his ghosts for the 20th century, with his short story *The Dust-Cloud* (1906) featuring perhaps one of the earliest ghost automobiles, and *The Confession of Charles Linkworth* (1912) demonstrating the haunting potential of the telephone.

This collection opens with James's *Casting the Runes* (first published in *More Ghost Stories of an Antiquary* in 1911) and Benson's *The Room in the Tower* (first published in *Pall Mall Magazine* in January 1912). Both stories include visions of the protagonist's fate (as either prophetic dreams or ominous warnings) as a plot device. This makes sound narrative sense

---

4   The 601st meeting of the Chit-Chat Club on 28th October 1893, where James read *Lost Hearts* and *Canon Alberic's Scrap-Book*.

for a Jamesian ghost story: the phantom has to slowly make its presence known, or else there will be no gradual rise in tension, no scares, and no story worth telling! But these premonitions also have a secondary narrative function: they warn the protagonist of the looming danger, thereby allowing him to evade his fate.

The use of prophetic visions as a story element raises interesting questions regarding free will and inevitability. In *The Room in the Tower*, was the protagonist free to escape his fate and refuse to enter the room, or was it inevitable? He seems to not even consider the possibility of refusal, and enters for reasons of social propriety; any desire he may have to flee is subordinated to the expectations of his host. In *Casting the Runes*, it initially appears that Karswell's curse is inevitable, and that a mere "*three months were allowed*" before each victim's demise. However, the portent of his fate leads Dunning to the one man with information that can help him, and ultimately his will to act allows him to escape the seemingly inexorable.

Of course, in a fictional world, there is only one will—that of the writer. But that will is also constrained by the wills of others: the will of the publisher, the will of the reader, the will of the critic, and the will of anyone making demands on the author's time or output. Our free will, if it exists at all, exists only in isolation; in reality, all of our actions are governed to varying degrees by various internal and external factors. Harrington's will to live is overruled by Karswell's desire to kill him; the protagonist's fear of the room in the tower is secondary to his social obligations. We may yet discover that the ability to predict the future or reconstruct the past does not require supernatural intervention, but merely a full understanding of the natural laws that govern our actions.

Mother Nature's Revenge

The Great War extracted a heavy toll not only from soldiers and civilians, but also from the natural world itself. The digging of trenches defaced the landscape of France and Belgium; it is estimated that 494,000 acres of French forest were destroyed, and the battle of the Somme alone left over 250,000 acres of farmland unfit for agriculture.[5] The use of chemical weapons was also devastating for the environment, with chlorine and phosgene gas clouds in particular killing everything in their path.[6] In addition, sixteen million horses and mules contributed to the war effort,[7] with an estimated 484,143 British horses, mules, camels and bullocks dying between 1914 and 1918. Man had declared war not only against man, but also against nature itself.

Man's affronts against nature may have been in the mind of Arthur Machen (Arthur Llewellyn Jones, 1863–1947) when he composed *The Terror*, a novel first published in 1917. In this collection, I have included an abridged version of the novel, named *The Coming of the Terror*, which was first published in the magazine *The Century*, also in 1917. The novel was written while the First World War was still raging, and it thus provides some insight into how the conflict was viewed in Britain at the time. In *The Coming of the Terror*, the

---

5   Susan D. Lanier-Graham. *The Ecology of War: Environmental Impacts of Weaponry and Warfare.* New York: Walker Publishing Company, Inc., 1993.

6   Robert Harris and Jeremy Paxton. *A Higher Form of Killing: The Secret History of Chemical and Biological Warfare.* New York: Random House, 2002.

7   Ernest Baynes. *Animal Heroes of the Great War.* New York: Macmillan, 1925.

mysterious attacks occurring in the British countryside are at first attributed to German spies, saboteurs, or secret weapons. It eventually becomes clear that it is not the Germans but the natural world itself that is responsible for the attacks, and although the protagonists propose several hypotheses to explain these phenomena, none of these are proven correct by the end. Ultimately, the true horror lies in man's impotent incomprehension of the unbridled forces of nature.

With the invention of fixed-wing airplanes, man stood poised to invade one of the final bastions of nature: the stratosphere. By 1913, an altitude record of 35,433 feet (10.8 km) had been set using a hot air balloon[8] and a record of 18,410 feet (5,610 m) had been set using a fixed-wing aircraft.[9] With airplanes continually setting new altitude records in the 1910s, it must have seemed clear to men of the time that the 40,000 foot barrier would eventually be breached. In *The Horror of the Heights*, a story very much of its time, the British author and physician Sir Arthur Conan Doyle (1859–1930) considered the possibility that an exotic ecosystem may exist above our heads in the recently discovered stratosphere. First published in the *The Strand Magazine* in November 1913, *The Horror of the Heights* suggests that man, in his arrogance and ignorance, is very much out of his element in the air.

The next story, *Unseen—Unfeared*, explores a side of nature that is as invisible to us as it is incomprehensible. First published in *People's Favorite Magazine* in 1919, *Unseen—Unfeared* was authored by Gertrude Barrows Bennett (1884–1948) under the pseudonym Francis Stevens. Bennett, an American author and stenographer, wrote a number of fantastical novels and short stories, including *The*

---

8   Set by Arthur Berson and Reinhard Süring in the hydrogen balloon Preuße on 31st July 1901.

9   Set by Roland Garros with a monoplane on 11th September 1912.

Citadel of Fear (1918) and *Claimed* (1920). Although very "Lovecraftian" in both tone and content, *Unseen—Unfeared* actually pre-dates all but the very earliest of H.P. Lovecraft's published works—and may have inspired Lovecraft's own story *From Beyond* (1934), which also explores the idea of invisible beings that inhabit a dimension that overlaps with our own. *Unseen—Unfeared* suggests that these beings (if they truly exist) are birthed from man's own evil thoughts, which must have seemed considerable in the wake of the First World War. This short story is also notable for including another theme that famously infuses much of Lovecraft's work: the fear and distrust of the alien. However, the revulsion felt by the protagonist in *Unseen—Unfeared* is an integral plot point, rather than just a reflection of the author's own fears or a device used to heighten the sense of isolation. As such, *Unseen—Unfeared* includes terms that readers in the 21st century may find offensive; the text has been presented as originally published in *People's Favorite Magazine.*

For the final story in this section we look to Howard Phillips Lovecraft (1890–1937) himself. Lovecraft's reputation as an ailurophile is well-known: he famously penned an essay of nearly 6000 words on why cats are better than dogs.[10] As such, it is not surprising that he would combine his affection for felines with his interest in the esoteric in his short story *The Cats of Ulthar*, which was first published in *The Tryout* in November 1920. This short yet satisfying tale of revenge exacted by the heirs of Bast has remained perennially popular, its assertion that the humble moggy is imbued with the dark and ancient mysteries of nature no doubt resonating with cat lovers.

---

10   H.P. Lovecraft. *Cats and Dogs. Something About Cats and Other Pieces*, Arkham House, 1949.

The Unsettled of Shape

In an age of total war, it is tempting to see one's enemies not as men, but as ravaging beasts. By persuading ourselves that those who commit heinous acts are animals, we are not forced to confront the darkness that lurks in our own hearts. This desire to distance ourselves from man's worst impulses may have given rise to accusations of lycanthropy in the European Middle Ages: in one famous case, that of the so-called Werewolf of Dole, a French hermit named Gilles Garnier was accused of killing and eating children; he confessed (perhaps under torture) to being a werewolf, and was burned at the stake on 18th January 1574. Although few believe in literal shapeshifting in our substantially more materialistic age, the legends continue to reflect fears of our own bestial side.

Here, I have included four stories that allude to shifters of shape, with the first originally published as the title story of the collection *Dracula's Guest and Other Weird Stories* in 1914. Authored by Abraham (Bram) Stoker (1847–1912) and published posthumously at the behest of his widow, Florence Stoker, née Balcombe (1858–1937), *Dracula's Guest* is famously an excised portion of the novel *Dracula* (1897), most likely the original first chapter. The protagonist, who may or may not be Jonathan Harker, is accosted by a large wolf, the true nature (*"A wolf—and yet not a wolf!"*) and intentions of which remain ambiguous. It may be the Count or one of his servants sent to protect Harker, or possibly the mysterious Countess Dolingen—or perhaps strangest of all—just a wolf.

The belief that witches can assume the shape of hares was once common throughout the British Isles, and was perhaps popularised by accusations of such during witch hunts in Early Modern Europe. However, the idea of shapeshifting witches is not confined to Britain and Ireland, for folktales of hags injured while in animal form (most commonly cats and

hares, but also other animals) can be found across Europe.[11]
The English author Bernard Capes (1854–1918) included *The
White Hare,* a version of the legend of the witch shot while in
animal form, in his short story collection *The Fabulists* (first
published in 1915). *The Fabulists* is framed as the stories of four
fictitious itinerant storytellers, named Raven, Duxbury, Scar-
rot, and Heriot, with Raven delivering *The White Hare.* Capes,
as Raven, understands that his intended audience is already
familiar with this folktale, and thus provides a unique twist.

This collection finishes with two tales of exotic, if equivocal,
"shapeshifting." The first is *The Haunted Pampero,* authored by
William Hope Hodgson (1877–1918) and originally published
in *The Premier Magazine* in 1916. Hodgson is arguably best
remembered for the weird fiction classic *The House on the Bor-
derland* (1908) and for *Carnacki, the Ghost-Finder* (1913), but
he also drew on his experiences as a sailor to pen many strange
stories of a nautical nature, including *The Haunted Pampero.*
The true nature of what haunts the *Pampero* is ultimately left
ambiguous—some versions of the text omit the final sentence,
an editorial decision perhaps taken to strengthen the supernatural interpretation at the expense of the psychological.

The final story in this collection is *The Middle Bedroom*
(first published in *The Novel Magazine* in December 1918),
by the Irish author and physician Henry De Vere Stacpoole
(1863–1951), who remains best known for penning *The Blue
Lagoon* (1908). The nature of the one-way transformation of
the bedroom's occupant is also open to interpretation, and perhaps best left in the reader's imagination. Ultimately, the story
serves as a cautionary tale against atomisation and alienation
from one's fellow man, lest the beast within find its way out.

---

11   Classified as Migratory Legends of Type 3055 "The Witch That Was
Hurt" in the system established by Norwegian folklorist Reidar Thoralf
Christiansen (1886–1971).

Days Gone By

In the words of Arthur Machen, "*...every man is the child of his age, however much he may hate it.*"[12] No writer is free from the influence of the age into which he or she is born, and, for better or worse, all fiction reflects the time in which it was written. To provide some historical context to the works collected here, each story is preceded by a short chronicle of historical events for the year in which it was published. Of course, the world is a large and complex place, and so the chronicles contained herein can only provide the briefest of insights into this tumultuous decade. Nevertheless, I hope they will help root the stories in their natural time.

I would like to extend my earnest thanks to the talented C. Raymond Hall for the wonderful illustrations commissioned for this collection; my dear family and friends for their tireless help in proofreading the draft; and everyone at Imprint Digital for their professional work in bringing this collection to printed life. And finally, I would like to thank you, gentle reader. I hope you enjoy these ten stories as much as I do, and I encourage you to seek out other works by the featured authors. The next book in this Glowbug series will reach back further into the past to present ten horror stories from the Edwardian era (1901–1910); I look forward to seeing you there.

D. Edward Wright
January 2024

---

12   Arthur Machen. *The Bowmen and Other Legends of the War*. G. P. Putnam's Sons, London, 1915.

Creepy
Tales of the
1910s

In the year 1911

3 Jan.	The Siege of Sidney Street: the police and army battle a Latvian gang in London.
27 April	The Second Canton Uprising against the Qing dynasty takes place in Guangzhou, China.
25 May	Mexican President Porfirio Díaz resigns, departing for Spain six days later.
31 May	Launch of the hull of the RMS *Titanic* into the mouth of the River Lagan in Belfast.
21 June	The RMS *Olympic*, captained by Edward Smith, arrives in New York at the end of her maiden voyage from Southampton.
22 June	Coronation of King George V and Queen Mary at Westminster Abbey, London.
24 July	Machu Picchu is discovered by American explorer and politician Hiram Bingham.
21 Aug.	The *Mona Lisa* is stolen from the Louvre by Italian art thief Vincenzo Peruggia.
29 Sept.	Italy declares war on the Ottoman Empire and invades Libya.
10 Oct.	Beginning of the Wuchang Uprising against the Qing dynasty in China.
1 Nov.	First reported instance of aerial bombardment using an airplane: Italian pilot Giulio Gavotti drops bombs from a monoplane onto an Ottoman military camp in Libya.
1 Dec.	Outer Mongolia declares independence from the Qing dynasty.
14 Dec.	Roald Amundsen's Norwegian expedition is the first to reach the geographical South Pole.
29 Dec.	Sun Yat-sen is elected Provisional President of the Republic of China.

Casting the Runes

M. R. James

> *"April 15th, 190–.*
>
> "DEAR SIR,—I am requested by the Council of the —
> Association to return to you the draft of a paper on *The Truth
> of Alchemy*, which you have been good enough to offer to
> read at our forthcoming meeting, and to inform you that the
> Council do not see their way to including it in the programme.
>
> > "I am,
> >
> > > "Yours faithfully,
> > >
> > > > "*— Secretary.*"

> *"April 18th.*
>
> "DEAR SIR,—I am sorry to say that my engagements do
> not permit of my affording you an interview on the subject
> of your proposed paper. Nor do our laws allow of your dis-
> cussing the matter with a Committee of our Council, as you
> suggest. Please allow me to assure you that the fullest consid-
> eration was given to the draft which you submitted, and that
> it was not declined without having been referred to the judge-
> ment of a most competent authority. No personal question
> (it can hardly be necessary for me to add) can have had the
> slightest influence on the decision of the Council.
>
> > "Believe me (*ut supra*)."

"*April 20th.*

"The Secretary of the — Association begs respectfully to inform Mr. Karswell that it is impossible for him to communicate the name of any person or persons to whom the draft of Mr. Karswell's paper may have been submitted; and further desires to intimate that he cannot undertake to reply to any further letters on this subject."

"And who *is* Mr. Karswell?" inquired the Secretary's wife. She had called at his office, and (perhaps unwarrantably) had picked up the last of these three letters, which the typist had just brought in.

"Why, my dear, just at present Mr. Karswell is a very angry man. But I don't know much about him otherwise, except that he is a person of wealth, his address is Lufford Abbey, Warwickshire, and he's an alchemist, apparently, and wants to tell us all about it; and that's about all—except that I don't want to meet him for the next week or two. Now, if you're ready to leave this place, I am."

"What have you been doing to make him angry?" asked Mrs. Secretary.

"The usual thing, my dear, the usual thing: he sent in a draft of a paper he wanted to read at the next meeting, and we referred it to Edward Dunning—almost the only man in England who knows about these things—and he said it was perfectly hopeless, so we declined it. So Karswell has been pelting me with letters ever since. The last thing he wanted was the name of the man we referred his nonsense to; you saw my answer to that. But don't you say anything about it, for goodness' sake."

"I should think not, indeed. Did I ever do such a thing? I do hope, though, he won't get to know that it was poor Mr. Dunning."

"Poor Mr. Dunning? I don't know why you call him that; he's a very happy man, is Dunning. Lots of hobbies and a comfortable home, and all his time to himself."

"I only meant I should be sorry for him if this man got hold of his name, and came and bothered him."

"Oh, ah! yes. I daresay he would be poor Mr. Dunning then."

The Secretary and his wife were lunching out, and the friends to whose house they were bound were Warwickshire people. So Mrs. Secretary had already settled it in her own mind that she would question them judiciously about Mr. Karswell. But she was saved the trouble of leading up to the subject, for the hostess said to the host, before many minutes had passed, "I saw the Abbot of Lufford this morning."

The host whistled. "*Did* you? What in the world brings him up to town?"

"Goodness knows; he was coming out of the British Museum gate as I drove past." It was not unnatural that Mrs. Secretary should inquire whether this was a real Abbot who was being spoken of. "Oh no, my dear: only a neighbour of ours in the country who bought Lufford Abbey a few years ago. His real name is Karswell."

"Is he a friend of yours?" asked Mr. Secretary, with a private wink to his wife.

The question let loose a torrent of declamation. There was really nothing to be said for Mr. Karswell. Nobody knew what he did with himself: his servants were a horrible set of people; he had invented a new religion for himself, and practised no one could tell what appalling rites; he was very easily offended, and never forgave anybody; he had a dreadful face (so the lady insisted, her husband somewhat demurring); he never did a kind action, and whatever influence he did exert was mischievous.

"Do the poor man justice, dear," the husband interrupted. "You forget the treat he gave the school children."

"Forget it, indeed! But I'm glad you mentioned it, because it gives an idea of the man. Now, Florence, listen to this. The first winter he was at Lufford this delightful neighbour of ours wrote to the clergyman of his parish (he's not ours, but we know him very well) and offered to show the school children some magic-lantern slides. He said he had some new kinds, which he thought would interest them. Well, the clergyman was rather surprised, because Mr. Karswell had shown himself inclined to be unpleasant to the children— complaining of their trespassing, or something of the sort; but of course he accepted, and the evening was fixed, and our friend went himself to see that everything went right. He said he never had been so thankful for anything as that his own children were all prevented from being there: they were at a children's party at our house, as a matter of fact. Because this Mr. Karswell had evidently set out with the intention of frightening these poor village children out of their wits, and I do believe, if he had been allowed to go on, he would actually have done so. He began with some comparatively mild things. Red Riding Hood was one, and even then, Mr. Farrer said, the wolf was so dreadful that several of the smaller children had to be taken out: and he said Mr. Karswell began the story by producing a noise like a wolf howling in the distance, which was the most gruesome thing he had ever heard. All the slides he showed, Mr. Farrer said, were most clever; they were absolutely realistic, and where he had got them or how he worked them he could not imagine. Well, the show went on, and the stories kept on becoming a little more terrifying each time, and the children were mesmerised into complete silence. At last he produced a series which represented a little boy passing through his own park—Lufford, I mean— in the evening. Every child in the room could recognize the place from the pictures. And this poor boy was followed, and at last pursued and overtaken, and either torn in pieces or somehow made away with, by a horrible hopping creature in white, which you saw first dodging about among the trees, and gradually it appeared more and more plainly. Mr. Farrer said it gave him one of the worst nightmares he ever remembered, and what it must have meant to the children doesn't bear thinking of. Of course this was too much, and he spoke very sharply indeed to Mr. Karswell, and said it couldn't go on. All *he* said was: 'Oh, you think it's time to bring our little show to an end and send them home to their beds? *Very well!*' and then, if you please, he switched on another slide, which showed a great mass of snakes, centipedes, and disgusting creatures with wings, and somehow or other he made it seem as if they were climbing out of the picture and getting in amongst the audience; and this was accompanied by a sort of dry rustling noise which sent the children nearly mad, and of course they stampeded. A good many of them were rather hurt in getting out of the room, and I don't suppose one of them closed an eye that night. There was the most dreadful trouble in the village afterwards. Of course the mothers threw a good part of the blame on poor Mr. Farrer, and, if they could have got past the gates, I believe the fathers would have broken every window in the Abbey. Well, now, that's Mr. Karswell: that's the Abbot of Lufford, my dear, and you can imagine how we covet *his* society."

"Yes, I think he has all the possibilities of a distinguished criminal, has Karswell," said the host. "I should be sorry for anyone who got into his bad books."

"Is he the man, or am I mixing him up with someone else?" asked the Secretary (who for some minutes had been wearing the frown of the man who is trying to recollect something). "Is he the man who brought out a 'History of Witchcraft' some time back—ten years or more?"

"That's the man; do you remember the reviews of it?"

"Certainly I do; and what's equally to the point, I knew the author of the most incisive of the lot. So did you: you must remember John Harrington; he was at John's in our time."

"Oh, very well indeed, though I don't think I saw or heard anything of him between the time I went down and the day I read the account of the inquest on him."

"Inquest?" said one of the ladies. "What has happened to him?"

"Why, what happened was that he fell out of a tree and broke his neck. But the puzzle was, what could have induced him to get up there. It was a mysterious business, I must say. Here was this man—not an athletic fellow, was he? and with no eccentric twist about him that was ever noticed—walking home along a country road late in the evening—no tramps about—well known and liked in the place—and he suddenly begins to run like mad, loses his hat and stick, and finally shins up a tree—quite a difficult tree—growing in the hedgerow: a dead branch gives way, and he comes down with it and breaks his neck, and there he's found next morning with the most dreadful face of fear on him that could be imagined. It was pretty evident, of course, that he had been chased by something, and people talked of savage dogs, and beasts escaped out of menageries; but there was nothing to be made of that. That was in '89, and I believe his brother Henry (whom I remember as well at Cambridge, but *you* probably don't) has been trying to get on the track of an explanation ever since. He, of course, insists there was malice in it, but I don't know. It's difficult to see how it could have come in."

After a time the talk reverted to the "History of Witchcraft." "Did you ever look into it?" asked the host.

"Yes, I did," said the Secretary. "I went so far as to read it."

"Was it as bad as it was made out to be?"

"Oh, in point of style and form, quite hopeless. It deserved all the pulverising it got. But, besides that, it was an evil book. The man believed every word of what he was saying, and I'm very much mistaken if he hadn't tried the greater part of his receipts."

"Well, I only remember Harrington's review of it, and I must say if I'd been the author it would have quenched my literary ambition for good. I should never have held up my head again."

"It hasn't had that effect in the present case. But come, it's half-past three; I must be off."

On the way home the Secretary's wife said, "I do hope that horrible man won't find out that Mr. Dunning had anything to do with the rejection of his paper."

"I don't think there's much chance of that," said the Secretary. "Dunning won't mention it himself, for these matters are confidential, and none of us will for the same reason. Karswell won't know his name, for Dunning hasn't published anything on the same subject yet. The only danger is that Karswell might find out, if he was to ask the British Museum people who was in the habit of consulting alchemical manuscripts: I can't very well tell them not to mention Dunning, can I? It would set them talking at once. Let's hope it won't occur to him."

However, Mr. Karswell was an astute man.

This much is in the way of prologue. On an evening rather later in the same week, Mr. Edward Dunning was returning from the British Museum, where he had been engaged in research, to the comfortable house in a suburb where he lived alone, tended by two excellent women who had been long with him. There is nothing to be added by way of description of him to what we have heard already. Let us follow him as he takes his sober course homewards.

A train took him to within a mile or two of his house, and an electric tram a stage farther. The line ended at a point some three hundred yards from his front door. He had had enough of reading when he got into the car, and indeed the light was not such as to allow him to do more than study the advertisements on the panes of glass that faced him as he sat. As was not unnatural, the advertisements in this particular line of cars were objects of his frequent contemplation, and, with the possible exception of the brilliant and convincing dialogue between Mr. Lamplough and an eminent K.C. on the subject of Pyretic Saline, none of them afforded much scope to his imagination. I am wrong: there was one at the corner of the car furthest from him which did not seem familiar. It was in blue letters on a yellow ground, and all that he could read of it was a name—John Harrington—and something like a date. It could be of no interest to him to know more; but for all that, as the car emptied, he was just curious enough to move along the seat until he could read it well. He felt to a slight extent repaid for his trouble; the advertisement was *not* of the usual type. It ran thus: "In memory of John Harrington, F.S.A., of The Laurels, Ashbrooke. Died Sept. 18th, 1889. Three months were allowed."

The car stopped. Mr. Dunning, still contemplating the blue letters on the yellow ground, had to be stimulated to rise by a word from the conductor.

"I beg your pardon," he said, "I was looking at that advertisement; it's a very odd one, isn't it?"

The conductor read it slowly. "Well, my word," he said, "I never see that one before. Well, that is a cure, ain't it? Someone bin up to their jokes 'ere, I should think." He got out a duster and applied it, not without saliva, to the pane and then to the outside. "No," he said, returning, "that ain't no transfer; seems to me as if it was reg'lar *in* the glass, what I mean in the substance, as you may say. Don't you think so, sir?"

Mr. Dunning examined it and rubbed it with his glove, and agreed. "Who looks after these advertisements, and gives leave for them to be put up? I wish you would inquire. I will just take a note of the words."

At this moment there came a call from the driver: "Look alive, George, time's up."

"All right, all right; there's somethink else what's up at this end. You come and look at this 'ere glass."

"What's gorn with the glass?" said the driver, approaching. "Well, and oo's 'Arrington? What's it all about?"

"I was just asking who was responsible for putting the advertisements up in your cars, and saying it would be as well to make some inquiry about this one."

"Well, sir, that's all done at the Company's orfice, that work is: it's our Mr. Timms, I believe, looks into that. When we put up tonight I'll leave word, and per'aps I'll be able to tell you tomorrer if you 'appen to be coming this way."

This was all that passed that evening. Mr Dunning did just go to the trouble of looking up Ashbrooke, and found that it was in Warwickshire.

Next day he went to town again. The car (it was the same car) was too full in the morning to allow of his getting a word with the conductor: he could only be sure that the curious advertisement had been made away with. The close of the day brought a further element of mystery into the transaction. He had missed the tram, or else preferred walking home, but at a rather late hour, while he was at work in his study, one of the maids came to say that two men from the tramways were very anxious to speak to him. This was a reminder of the advertisement, which he had, he says, nearly forgotten. He had the men in—they were the conductor and driver of the car—and when the matter of refreshment had been attended to, asked what Mr. Timms had had to say about the advertisement.

"Well, sir, that's what we took the liberty to step round about," said the conductor. "Mr. Timms 'e give William 'ere the rough side of his tongue about that: 'cordin' to 'im there warn't no advertisement of that description sent in, nor ordered, nor paid for, nor put up, nor nothink, let alone not bein' there, and we was playing the fool takin' up his time. 'Well,' I says, 'if that's the case, all I ask of you, Mr. Timms,' I says, 'is to take and look at it for yourself,' I says. 'Of course if it ain't there,' I says, 'you may take and call me what you like.' 'Right,' he says, 'I will': and we went straight off. Now, I leave it to you, sir, if that ad., as we term 'em, with 'Arrington on it warn't as plain as ever you see anythink—blue letters on yeller glass, and as I says at the time, and you borne me out, reg'lar in the glass, because, if you remember, you recollect of me swabbing it with my duster."

"To be sure I do, quite clearly—well?"

"You may say well, I don't think. Mr. Timms he gets in that car with a light—no, he telled William to 'old the light outside. 'Now,' he says, 'where's your precious ad. what we've 'eard so much about?' ' 'Ere it is,' I says, 'Mr. Timms,' and I laid my 'and on it." The conductor paused.

"Well," said Mr. Dunning, "it was gone, I suppose. Broken?"

"Broke!—not it. There warn't, if you'll believe me, no more trace of them letters—blue letters they was—on that piece o' glass, than—well, it's no good *me* talkin'. *I* never see such a thing. I leave it to William here if—but there, as I says, where's the benefit in me going on about it?"

"And what did Mr. Timms say?"

"Why 'e did what I give 'im leave to—called us pretty much anythink he liked, and I don't know as I blame him so much neither. But what we thought, William and me did, was as we seen you take down a bit of a note about that—well, that letterin'—"

"I certainly did that, and I have it now. Did you wish me to speak to Mr. Timms myself, and show it to him? Was that what you came in about?"

"There, didn't I say as much?" said William. "Deal with a gent if you can get on the track of one, that's my word. Now perhaps, George, you'll allow as I ain't took you very far wrong tonight."

"Very well, William, very well; no need for you to go on as if you'd 'ad to frog's-march me 'ere. I come quiet, didn't I?

All the same for that, we 'adn't ought to take up your time this way, sir; but if it so 'appened you could find time to step round to the Company's orfice in the morning and tell Mr. Timms what you seen for yourself, we should lay under a very 'igh obligation to you for the trouble. You see it ain't bein' called— well, one thing and another, as we mind, but if they got it into their 'ead at the orfice as we seen things as warn't there, why, one thing leads to another, and where we should be a twelve-munce 'ence—well, you can understand what I mean."

Amid further elucidations of the proposition, George, conducted by William, left the room.

The incredulity of Mr. Timms (who had a nodding acquaintance with Mr. Dunning) was greatly modified on the following day by what the latter could tell and show him; and any bad mark that might have been attached to the names of William and George was not suffered to remain on the Company's books; but explanation there was none.

Mr. Dunning's interest in the matter was kept alive by an incident of the following afternoon. He was walking from his club to the train, and he noticed some way ahead a man with a handful of leaflets such as are distributed to passers-by by agents of enterprising firms. This agent had not chosen a very crowded street for his operations: in fact, Mr. Dunning did not see him get rid of a single leaflet before he himself reached the spot. One was thrust into his hand as he passed: the hand that gave it touched his, and he experienced a sort of little shock as it did so. It seemed unnaturally rough and hot. He looked in passing at the giver, but the impression he got was so unclear that, however much he tried to reckon it up subsequently, nothing would come. He was walking quickly, and as he went on glanced at the paper. It was a blue one. The name of Harrington in large capitals caught his eye. He stopped, startled, and felt for his glasses. The next instant the leaflet was twitched out of his hand by a man who hurried past, and was irrecoverably gone. He ran back a few paces, but where was the passer-by? and where the distributor?

It was in a somewhat pensive frame of mind that Mr. Dunning passed on the following day into the Select Manuscript Room of the British Museum, and filled up tickets for Harley 3586, and some other volumes. After a few minutes they were brought to him, and he was settling the one he wanted first upon the desk, when he thought he heard his own name whispered behind him. He turned round hastily, and, in doing so, brushed his little portfolio of loose papers on to the floor. He saw no one he recognized except one of the staff in charge of the room, who nodded to him, and he proceeded to pick up his papers. He thought he had them all, and was turning to begin work, when a stout gentleman at the table behind him, who was just rising to leave, and had collected his own belongings, touched him on the shoulder, saying, "May I give you this? I think it should be yours," and handed him a missing quire.

"It is mine, thank you," said Mr. Dunning. In another moment the man had left the room. Upon finishing his work for the afternoon, Mr. Dunning had some conversation with the assistant in charge, and took occasion to ask who the stout gentleman was.

"Oh, he's a man named Karswell," said the assistant; "he was asking me a week ago who were the great authorities on alchemy, and of course I told him you were the only one in the country. I'll see if I can catch him: he'd like to meet you, I'm sure."

"For heaven's sake don't dream of it!" said Mr. Dunning, "I'm particularly anxious to avoid him."

"Oh! very well," said the assistant, "he doesn't come here often: I daresay you won't meet him."

More than once on the way home that day Mr. Dunning confessed to himself that he did not look forward with his usual cheerfulness to a solitary evening. It seemed to him that something ill-defined and impalpable had stepped in between him and his fellow-men—had taken him in charge, as it were. He wanted to sit close up to his neighbours in the train and in the tram, but as luck would have it both train and car were markedly empty. The conductor George was thoughtful, and appeared to be absorbed in calculations as to the number of passengers. On arriving at his house he found Dr. Watson, his medical man, on his doorstep.

"I've had to upset your household arrangements, I'm sorry to say, Dunning. Both your servants *hors de combat*. In fact, I've had to send them to the Nursing Home."

"Good heavens! what's the matter?"

"It's something like ptomaine poisoning, I should think: you've not suffered yourself, I can see, or you wouldn't be walking about. I think they'll pull through all right."

"Dear, dear! Have you any idea what brought it on?"

"Well, they tell me they bought some shellfish from a hawker at their dinner-time. It's odd. I've made inquiries, but I can't find that any hawker has been to other houses in the street. I couldn't send word to you; they won't be back for a bit yet. You come and dine with me tonight, anyhow, and we can make arrangements for going on. Eight o'clock. Don't be too anxious."

The solitary evening was thus obviated; at the expense of some distress and inconvenience, it is true. Mr. Dunning spent the time pleasantly enough with the doctor (a rather recent settler), and returned to his lonely home at about 11:30. The night he passed is not one on which he looks back with any satisfaction. He was in bed and the light was out. He was wondering if the charwoman would come early enough to get him hot water next morning, when he heard the unmistakable sound of his study door opening. No step followed it on the passage floor, but the sound must mean mischief, for he knew that he had shut the door that evening after putting his papers away in his desk. It was rather shame than courage that induced him to slip out into the passage and lean over the banister in his nightgown, listening. No light was visible; no further sound came: only a gust of warm, or even hot air played for an instant round his shins. He went back and decided to lock himself into his room. There was more unpleasantness, however. Either an economical suburban company had decided that their light would not be required in the small hours, and had stopped working, or else something was wrong with the meter; the effect was in any case that the electric light was off. The obvious course was to find a match, and also to consult his watch: he might as well know how many hours of discomfort awaited him. So he put his hand into the well-known nook under the pillow: only, it did not get so far.

What he touched was, according to his account, a mouth, with teeth, and with hair about it, and, he declares, not the mouth of a human being. I do not think it is any use to guess what he said or did; but he was in a spare room with the door locked and his ear to it before he was clearly conscious again. And there he spent the rest of a most miserable night, looking every moment for some fumbling at the door: but nothing came.

The venturing back to his own room in the morning was attended with many listenings and quiverings. The door stood open, fortunately, and the blinds were up (the servants had been out of the house before the hour of drawing them down); there was, to be short, no trace of an inhabitant. The watch, too, was in its usual place; nothing was disturbed, only the wardrobe door had swung open, in accordance with its confirmed habit. A ring at the back door now announced the charwoman, who had been ordered the night before, and nerved Mr. Dunning, after letting her in, to continue his search in other parts of the house. It was equally fruitless.

The day thus begun went on dismally enough. He dared not go to the Museum: in spite of what the assistant had said, Karswell might turn up there, and Dunning felt he could not cope with a probably hostile stranger. His own house was odious; he hated sponging on the doctor. He spent some little time in a call at the Nursing Home, where he was slightly cheered by a good report of his housekeeper and maid. Towards lunch-time he betook himself to his club, again experiencing a gleam of satisfaction at seeing the Secretary of the Association. At luncheon Dunning told his friend the more material of his woes, but could not bring himself to speak of those that weighed most heavily on his spirits.

"My poor dear man," said the Secretary, "what an upset! Look here: we're alone at home, absolutely. You must put up with us. Yes! no excuse: send your things in this afternoon." Dunning was unable to stand out: he was, in truth, becoming acutely anxious, as the hours went on, as to what that night might have waiting for him. He was almost happy as he hurried home to pack up.

His friends, when they had time to take stock of him, were rather shocked at his lorn appearance, and did their best to keep him up to the mark. Not altogether without success: but, when the two men were smoking alone later, Dunning became dull again.

Suddenly he said, "Gayton, I believe that alchemist man knows it was I who got his paper rejected."

Gayton whistled. "What makes you think that?" he said.

Dunning told of his conversation with the Museum assistant, and Gayton could only agree that the guess seemed likely to be correct. "Not that I care much," Dunning went on, "only it might be a nuisance if we were to meet. He's a bad-tempered party, I imagine."

Conversation dropped again; Gayton became more and more strongly impressed with the desolateness that came over Dunning's face and bearing, and finally—though with a considerable effort—he asked him point-blank whether something serious was not bothering him.

Dunning gave an exclamation of relief. "I was perishing to get it off my mind," he said. "Do you know anything about a man named John Harrington?"

Gayton was thoroughly startled, and at the moment could only ask why. Then the complete story of Dunning's experiences came out—what had happened in the tramcar, in his own house, and in the street, the troubling of spirit that had crept over him, and still held him; and he ended with the question he had begun with. Gayton was at a loss how to answer him. To tell the story of Harrington's end would perhaps be right; only, Dunning was in a nervous state, the story was a grim one, and he could not help asking himself whether there were not a connecting link between these two cases, in the person of Karswell. It was a difficult concession for a scientific man, but it could be eased by the phrase "hypnotic suggestion." In the end he decided that his answer tonight should be guarded; he would talk the situation over with his wife. So he said that he had known Harrington at Cambridge, and believed he had died suddenly in 1889, adding a few details about the man and his published work. He did talk over the matter with Mrs. Gayton, and, as he had anticipated, she leapt at once to the conclusion which had been hovering before him. It was she who reminded him of the surviving brother, Henry Harrington, and she also who suggested that he might be got hold of by means of their hosts of the day before.

"He might be a hopeless crank," objected Gayton.

"That could be ascertained from the Bennetts, who knew him," Mrs. Gayton retorted; and she undertook to see the Bennetts the very next day.

It is not necessary to tell in further detail the steps by which Henry Harrington and Dunning were brought together.

The next scene that requires to be narrated is a conversation that took place between the two. Dunning had told Harrington of the strange ways in which the dead man's name had been brought before him, and had said something, besides, of his own subsequent experiences. Then he had asked if Harrington was disposed, in return, to recall any of the circumstances connected with his brother's death. It is not necessary to dwell on Harrington's surprise at what he had heard: but his reply was readily given.

"John," he said, "was in a very odd state, undeniably, from time to time, during some weeks before, though not immediately before, the catastrophe. There were several things—the principal notion he had was that he thought he was being followed. No doubt he was an impressionable man, but he never had had such fancies as this before. I cannot get it out of my mind that there was ill-will at work, and what you tell me about yourself reminds me very much of my brother. Can you think of any possible connecting link?"

"There is just one that has been taking shape vaguely in my mind. I've been told that your brother reviewed a book very severely not long before he died, and just lately I have happened to cross the path of the man who wrote that book in a way he would resent."

"Don't tell me the man was called Karswell."

"Why not? that is exactly his name."

Henry Harrington leant back. "That is final to my mind. Now I must explain further. From something he said, I feel sure that my brother John was beginning to believe—very much against his will—that Karswell was at the bottom of his trouble. I want to tell you what seems to me to have a bearing on the situation. My brother was a great musician, and used to run up to concerts in town. He came back, three months before he died, from one of these, and gave me his programme to look at—an analytical programme: he always kept them. 'I nearly missed this one,' he said. 'I suppose I must have dropped it: anyhow, I was looking for it under my seat and in my pockets and so on, and my neighbour offered me his: said "might he give it me, he had no further use for it," and he went away just afterwards. I don't know who he was—a stout, clean-shaven man. I should have been sorry to miss it; of course I could have bought another, but this cost me nothing.' At another time he told me that he had been very uncomfortable both on the way to his hotel and during the night. I piece things together now in thinking it over. Then, not very long after, he was going over these programmes, putting them in order to have them bound up, and in this particular one (which by the way I had hardly glanced at), he found quite near the beginning a strip of paper with some very odd writing on it in red and black—most carefully done—it looked to me more like Runic letters than anything else. 'Why,' he said, 'this must belong to my fat neighbour. It looks as if it might be worth returning to him; it may be a copy of something; evidently someone has taken trouble over it. How can I find his address?' We talked it over for a little and agreed that it wasn't worth advertising about, and that my brother had better look out for the man at the next concert, to which he was going very soon. The paper was lying on the book and we were both by the fire; it was a cold, windy summer evening. I suppose the door blew open, though I didn't notice it: at any rate a gust—a warm gust it was—came quite suddenly between us, took the paper and blew it straight into the fire: it was light, thin paper, and flared and went up the chimney in a single ash. 'Well,' I said, 'you can't give it back now.' He said nothing for a minute: then rather crossly, 'No, I can't; but why you should keep on saying so I don't know.' I remarked that I didn't say it more than once. 'Not more than four times, you mean,' was all he said. I remember all that very clearly, without any good reason; and now to come to the point. I don't know if you looked at that book of Karswell's which my unfortunate brother reviewed. It's not likely that you should: but I did, both before his death and after it. The first time we made game of it together. It was written in no style at all—split infinitives, and every sort of thing that makes an Oxford gorge rise. Then there was nothing that the man didn't swallow: mixing up classical myths, and stories out of the *Golden Legend* with reports of savage customs of today—all very proper, no doubt, if you know how to use them, but he didn't: he seemed to put the *Golden Legend* and the *Golden Bough* exactly on a par, and to believe both: a pitiable exhibition, in short. Well, after the misfortune, I looked over the book again. It was no better than before, but the impression which it left this time on my mind was different. I suspected—as I told you—that Karswell had borne ill-will to my brother—even that he was in some way responsible for what had happened—and now his book seemed to me to be a very sinister performance indeed. One chapter in particular struck me, in which he spoke of 'casting the Runes' on people, either for the purpose of gaining their affection or of getting them out of the way—perhaps more especially the latter: he spoke of all this in a way that really seemed to me to imply actual knowledge. I've not time to go into details, but the upshot is that I am pretty sure from information received that the civil man at the concert was Karswell: I suspect—I more than suspect—that the paper was of importance: and I do believe that if my brother had been able to give it back, he might have been alive now. Therefore, it occurs to me to ask you whether you have anything to put beside what I have told you."

By way of answer, Dunning had the episode in the Manuscript Room at the British Museum to relate.

"Then he did actually hand you some papers; have you examined them? No? because we must, if you'll allow it, look at them at once, and very carefully."

They went to the still empty house—empty, for the two servants were not yet able to return to work. Dunning's portfolio of papers was gathering dust on the writing-table. In it were the quires of small-sized scribbling paper which he used for his transcripts: and from one of these, as he took it up, there slipped and fluttered out into the room with uncanny quickness, a strip of thin light paper. The window was open, but Harrington slammed it to, just in time to intercept the paper, which he caught. "I thought so," he said; "it might be the identical thing that was given to my brother. You'll have to look out, Dunning; this may mean something quite serious for you."

A long consultation took place. The paper was narrowly examined. As Harrington had said, the characters on it were more like Runes than anything else, but not decipherable by either man, and both hesitated to copy them, for fear, as they confessed, of perpetuating whatever evil purpose they might conceal. So it has remained impossible (if I may anticipate a little) to ascertain what was conveyed in this curious message or commission. Both Dunning and Harrington are firmly convinced that it had the effect of bringing its possessors into very undesirable company. That it must be returned to the source whence it came they were agreed, and further, that the only safe and certain way was that of personal service; and here contrivance would be necessary, for Dunning was known by sight to Karswell. He must, for one thing, alter his appearance by shaving his beard. But then might not the blow fall first? Harrington thought they could time it. He knew the date of the concert at which the "black spot" had been put on his brother: it was June 18th. The death had followed on Sept. 18th. Dunning reminded him that three months had been mentioned on the inscription on the car-window.

"Perhaps," he added, with a cheerless laugh, "mine may be a bill at three months too. I believe I can fix it by my diary. Yes, April 23rd was the day at the Museum; that brings us to July 23rd. Now, you know, it becomes extremely important to me to know anything you will tell me about the progress of your brother's trouble, if it is possible for you to speak of it."

"Of course. Well, the sense of being watched whenever he was alone was the most distressing thing to him. After a time

I took to sleeping in his room, and he was the better for that: still, he talked a great deal in his sleep. What about? Is it wise to dwell on that, at least before things are straightened out? I think not, but I can tell you this: two things came for him by post during those weeks, both with a London postmark, and addressed in a commercial hand. One was a woodcut of Bewick's, roughly torn out of the page: one which shows a moonlit road and a man walking along it, followed by an awful demon creature. Under it were written the lines out of the 'Ancient Mariner' (which I suppose the cut illustrates) about one who, having once looked round—

> 'Walks on, and turns no more his head,
> Because he knows a grisly fiend doth close behind him tread.'

The other was a calendar, such as tradesmen often send. My brother paid no attention to this, but I looked at it after his death, and found that everything after Sept. 18 had been torn out. You may be surprised at his having gone out alone the evening he was killed, but the fact is that during the last ten days or so of his life he had been quite free from the sense of being followed or watched."

The end of the consultation was this. Harrington, who knew a neighbour of Karswell's, thought he saw a way of keeping a watch on his movements. It would be Dunning's part to be in readiness to try to cross Karswell's path at any moment, to keep the paper safe and in a place of ready access.

They parted. The next weeks were no doubt a severe strain upon Dunning's nerves: the intangible barrier which had seemed to rise about him on the day when he received the paper, gradually developed into a brooding blackness that cut him off from all the means of escape to which one might have thought he would resort. No one was at hand who was likely to suggest them to him, and he seemed robbed of all initiative.

He waited with inexpressible anxiety as May, June, and early July passed on, for a mandate from Harrington. But all this time Karswell remained immovable at Lufford.

At last, in less than a week before the date he had come to look upon as the end of his earthly activities, came a telegram: "*Leaves Victoria by boat train Thursday night. Do not miss. I come to you tonight. Harrington.*"

He arrived accordingly, and they concocted plans. The train left Victoria at nine and its last stop before Dover was Croydon West. Harrington would mark down Karswell at Victoria, and look out for Dunning at Croydon, calling to him if need were by a name agreed upon. Dunning, disguised as far as might be, was to have no label or initials on any hand luggage, and must at all costs have the paper with him.

Dunning's suspense as he waited on the Croydon platform I need not attempt to describe. His sense of danger during the last days had only been sharpened by the fact that the cloud about him had perceptibly been lighter; but relief was an ominous symptom, and, if Karswell eluded him now, hope was gone: and there were so many chances of that. The rumour of the journey might be itself a device. The twenty minutes in which he paced the platform and persecuted every porter with inquiries as to the boat train were as bitter as any he had spent. Still, the train came, and Harrington was at the window. It was important, of course, that there should be no recognition: so Dunning got in at the further end of the corridor carriage, and only gradually made his way to the compartment where Harrington and Karswell were. He was pleased, on the whole, to see that the train was far from full.

Karswell was on the alert, but gave no sign of recognition. Dunning took the seat not immediately facing him, and attempted, vainly at first, then with increasing command of his faculties, to reckon the possibilities of making the desired transfer. Opposite to Karswell, and next to Dunning, was a heap of Karswell's coats on the seat. It would be of no use to slip the paper into these—he would not be safe, or would not feel so, unless in some way it could be proffered by him and accepted by the other. There was a handbag, open, and with papers in it. Could he manage to conceal this (so that perhaps Karswell might leave the carriage without it), and then find and give it to him? This was the plan that suggested itself. If he could only have counselled with Harrington! but that could not be. The minutes went on. More than once Karswell rose and went out into the corridor. The second time Dunning was on the point of attempting to make the bag fall off the seat, but he caught Harrington's eye, and read in it a warning.

Karswell, from the corridor, was watching: probably to see if the two men recognized each other. He returned, but was evidently restless: and, when he rose the third time, hope dawned, for something did slip off his seat and fall with hardly a sound to the floor. Karswell went out once more, and passed out of range of the corridor window. Dunning picked up what had fallen, and saw that the key was in his hands in the form of one of Cook's ticket-cases, with tickets in it. These cases have a pocket in the cover, and within very few seconds the paper of which we have heard was in the pocket of this one. To make the operation more secure, Harrington stood in the doorway of the compartment and fiddled with the blind. It was done, and done at the right time, for the train was now slowing down towards Dover.

In a moment more Karswell re-entered the compartment. As he did so, Dunning, managing, he knew not how, to suppress the tremble in his voice, handed him the ticket-case, saying, "May I give you this, sir? I believe it is yours."

After a brief glance at the ticket inside, Karswell uttered the hoped-for response, "Yes, it is; much obliged to you, sir," and he placed it in his breast pocket.

Even in the few moments that remained—moments of tense anxiety, for they knew not to what a premature finding of the paper might lead—both men noticed that the carriage seemed to darken about them and to grow warmer; that Karswell was fidgety and oppressed; that he drew the heap of loose coats near to him and cast it back as if it repelled him; and that he then sat upright and glanced anxiously at both. They, with sickening anxiety, busied themselves in collecting their belongings; but they both thought that Karswell was on the point of speaking when the train stopped at Dover Town. It was natural that in the short space between town and pier they should both go into the corridor.

At the pier they got out, but so empty was the train that they were forced to linger on the platform until Karswell should have passed ahead of them with his porter on the way to the boat, and only then was it safe for them to exchange a pressure of the hand and a word of concentrated congratulation. The effect upon Dunning was to make him almost faint. Harrington made him lean up against the wall, while he himself went forward a few yards within sight of the gangway to the boat, at which Karswell had now arrived. The man at the head of it examined his ticket, and, laden with coats, he passed down into the boat.

Suddenly the official called after him, "You, sir, beg pardon, did the other gentleman show his ticket?"

"What the devil do you mean by the other gentleman?" Karswell's snarling voice called back from the deck.

The man bent over and looked at him. "The devil? Well, I don't know, I'm sure," Harrington heard him say to himself, and then aloud, "My mistake, sir; must have been your rugs! ask your pardon." And then, to a subordinate near him, " 'Ad he got a dog with him, or what? Funny thing: I could 'a' swore 'e wasn't alone. Well, whatever it was, they'll 'ave to see to it aboard. She's off now. Another week and we shall be gettin' the 'oliday customers."

In five minutes more there was nothing but the lessening lights of the boat, the long line of the Dover lamps, the night breeze, and the moon.

Long and long the two sat in their room at the "Lord Warden." In spite of the removal of their greatest anxiety, they were oppressed with a doubt, not of the lightest. Had they been justified in sending a man to his death, as they believed they had? Ought they not to warn him, at least?

"No," said Harrington; "if he is the murderer I think him, we have done no more than is just. Still, if you think it better— but how and where can you warn him?"

"He was booked to Abbeville only," said Dunning. "I saw that. If I wired to the hotels there in Joanne's Guide, 'Examine your ticket-case, Dunning,' I should feel happier. This is the 21st: he will have a day. But I am afraid he has gone into the dark." So telegrams were left at the hotel office.

It is not clear whether these reached their destination, or whether, if they did, they were understood. All that is known is that, on the afternoon of the 23rd, an English traveller, examining the front of St Wulfram's Church at Abbeville, then under extensive repair, was struck on the head and instantly killed by a stone falling from the scaffold erected round the south-western tower, there being, as was clearly proved, no workman on the scaffold at that moment: and the traveller's papers identified him as Mr. Karswell.

Only one detail shall be added. At Karswell's sale a set of Bewick, sold with all faults, was acquired by Harrington. The page with the woodcut of the traveller and the demon was, as he had expected, mutilated. Also, after a judicious interval, Harrington repeated to Dunning something of what he had heard his brother say in his sleep: but it was not long before Dunning stopped him.

In the year 1912

1 Jan.	The Republic of China is established.
6 Jan.	New Mexico becomes the 47th state of the USA.
17 Jan.	Robert Falcon Scott and four other members of the British Terra Nova Expedition reach the South Pole, one month after Roald Amundsen.
12 Feb.	The Xuantong Emperor (Puyi) abdicates, marking the end of the Qing dynasty.
14 Feb.	Arizona becomes the 48th state of the USA.
1 March	Suffragettes led by Emmeline Pankhurst smash shop windows across London.
17 March	Lawrence Oates of the Terra Nova Expedition leaves his tent to face certain death in a blizzard, his final words: "I am just going outside and may be some time."
14–15 April	The RMS *Titanic* hits an iceberg and sinks in the Atlantic Ocean during its maiden voyage from Southampton to New York City.
20 April	Irish author Bram Stoker dies in London.
6 July	Opening ceremony of the 1912 Summer Olympics in Stockholm, Sweden.
30 July	Emperor Meiji of Japan dies at Meiji Palace in Tokyo. He is succeeded by his son Yoshihito, who reigns as the Taishō Emperor.
8 Oct.	Montenegro declares war on the Ottoman Empire, initiating the First Balkan War.
18 Oct.	Italy and the Ottoman Empire sign a treaty in Ouchy near Lausanne, Switzerland, ending the Italo-Turkish War.
5 Nov.	Woodrow Wilson wins the US Presidential Election, defeating incumbent William Howard Taft.

— 1912 —

The Room in the Tower

E. F. Benson

It is probable that everybody who is at all a constant dreamer has had at least one experience of an event or a sequence of circumstances which have come to his mind in sleep being subsequently realized in the material world. But, in my opinion, so far from this being a strange thing, it would be far odder if this fulfilment did not occasionally happen, since our dreams are, as a rule, concerned with people whom we know and places with which we are familiar, such as might very naturally occur in the awake and daylit world. True, these dreams are often broken into by some absurd and fantastic incident, which puts them out of court in regard to their subsequent fulfilment, but on the mere calculation of chances, it does not appear in the least unlikely that a dream imagined by anyone who dreams constantly should occasionally come true. Not long ago, for instance, I experienced such a fulfilment of a dream which seems to me in no way remarkable and to have no kind of psychical significance. The manner of it was as follows.

A certain friend of mine, living abroad, is amiable enough to write to me about once in a fortnight. Thus, when fourteen days or thereabouts have elapsed since I last heard from him, my mind, probably, either consciously or subconsciously, is expectant of a letter from him. One night last week I dreamed that as I was going upstairs to dress for dinner I heard, as I often heard, the sound of the postman's knock on my front door, and diverted my direction downstairs instead. There, among other correspondence, was a letter from him. Thereafter the fantastic entered, for on opening it I found inside the ace of diamonds, and scribbled across it in his well-known handwriting, "I am sending you this for safe custody, as you know it is running an unreasonable risk to keep aces in Italy." The next evening I was just preparing to go upstairs to dress when I heard the postman's knock, and did precisely as I had done in my dream. There, among other letters, was one from my friend. Only it did not contain the ace of diamonds. Had it done so, I should have attached more weight to the matter, which, as it stands, seems to me a perfectly ordinary coincidence. No doubt I consciously or subconsciously expected a letter from him, and this suggested to me my dream. Similarly, the fact that my friend had not written to me for a fortnight suggested to him that he should do so. But occasionally it is not so easy to find such an explanation, and for the following story I can find no explanation at all. It came out of the dark, and into the dark it has gone again.

All my life I have been a habitual dreamer: the nights are few, that is to say, when I do not find on awaking in the morning that some mental experience has been mine, and sometimes, all night long, apparently, a series of the most dazzling adventures befall me. Almost without exception these adventures are pleasant, though often merely trivial. It is of an exception that I am going to speak.

It was when I was about sixteen that a certain dream first came to me, and this is how it befell. It opened with my being set down at the door of a big red-brick house, where, I understood, I was going to stay. The servant who opened the door told me that tea was going on in the garden, and led me through a low dark-panelled hall, with a large open fireplace, on to a cheerful green lawn set round with flower beds. There were grouped about the tea-table a small party of people, but they were all strangers to me except one, who was a school-fellow called Jack Stone, clearly the son of the house, and he introduced me to his mother and father and a couple of sisters. I was, I remember, somewhat astonished to find myself here, for the boy in question was scarcely known to me, and I rather disliked what I knew of him: moreover, he had left school nearly a year before. The afternoon was very hot, and an intolerable oppression reigned. On the far side of the lawn ran a red-brick wall, with an iron gate in its centre, outside which stood a walnut tree. We sat in the shadow of the house opposite a row of long windows, inside which I could see a table with cloth laid, glimmering with glass and silver. This garden front of the house was very long, and at one end of it stood a tower of three stories, which looked to me much older than the rest of the building.

Before long, Mrs. Stone, who, like the rest of the party, had sat in absolute silence, said to me, "Jack will show you your room: I have given you the room in the tower."

Quite inexplicably my heart sank at her words. I felt as if I had known that I should have the room in the tower, and that it contained something dreadful and significant. Jack instantly got up, and I understood that I had to follow him. In silence we passed through the hall, and mounted a great oak staircase with many corners, and arrived at a small landing with two doors set in it. He pushed one of these open for me to enter, and without coming in himself, closed it behind me. Then I knew that my conjecture had been right: there was something awful in the room, and with the terror of nightmare growing swiftly and enveloping me, I awoke in a spasm of terror.

Now that dream or variations on it occurred to me intermittently for fifteen years. Most often it came in exactly this form, the arrival, the tea laid out on the lawn, the deadly silence succeeded by that one deadly sentence, the mounting with Jack Stone up to the room in the tower where horror dwelt, and it always came to a close in the nightmare of terror at that which was in the room, though I never saw what it was. At other times I experienced variations on this same theme. Occasionally, for instance, we would be sitting at dinner in the dining-room, into the windows of which I had looked on the first night when the dream of this house visited me, but wherever we were, there was the same silence, the same sense of dreadful oppression and foreboding. And the silence I knew would always be broken by Mrs. Stone saying to me, "Jack will show you your room: I have given you the room in the tower." Upon which (this was invariable) I had to follow him up the oak staircase with many corners, and enter the place that I dreaded more and more each time that I visited it in sleep. Or, again, I would find myself playing cards still in silence in a drawing-room lit with immense chandeliers, that gave a blinding illumination. What the game was I have no idea; what I remember, with a sense of miserable anticipation, was that soon Mrs. Stone would get up and say to me, "Jack will show you your room: I have given you the room in the tower." This drawing-room where we played cards was next to the dining-room, and, as I have said, was always brilliantly illuminated, whereas the rest of the house was full of dusk and shadows. And yet, how often, in spite of those bouquets of lights, have I not pored over the cards that were dealt to me, scarcely able for some reason to see them. Their designs, too, were strange: there were no red suits, but all were black, and among them there were certain cards which were black all over. I hated and dreaded those.

As this dream continued to recur, I got to know the greater part of the house. There was a smoking-room beyond the drawing-room, at the end of a passage with a green baize door. It was always very dark there, and as often as I went there I passed somebody whom I could not see in the doorway coming out. Curious developments, too, took place in the characters that peopled the dream as might happen to living persons. Mrs. Stone, for instance, who, when I first saw her, had been black haired, became grey, and instead of rising briskly, as she had done at first when she said, "Jack will show you your room: I have given you the room in the tower," got up very feebly, as if the strength was leaving her limbs. Jack also grew up, and became a rather ill-looking young man, with a brown moustache, while one of the sisters ceased to appear, and I understood she was married.

Then it so happened that I was not visited by this dream for six months or more, and I began to hope, in such inexplicable dread did I hold it, that it had passed away for good. But one night after this interval I again found myself being shown out on to the lawn for tea, and Mrs. Stone was not there, while the others were all dressed in black. At once I guessed the reason, and my heart leaped at the thought that perhaps this time I should not have to sleep in the room in the tower, and though we usually all sat in silence, on this occasion the sense of relief made me talk and laugh as I had never yet done. But even then matters were not altogether comfortable, for no one else spoke, but they all looked secretly at each other. And soon the foolish stream of my talk ran dry, and gradually an apprehension worse than anything I had previously known gained on me as the light slowly faded.

Suddenly a voice which I knew well broke the stillness, the voice of Mrs. Stone, saying, "Jack will show you your room: I have given you the room in the tower." It seemed to come from near the gate in the red-brick wall that bounded the lawn, and looking up, I saw that the grass outside was sown thick with gravestones. A curious greyish light shone from them, and I could read the lettering on the grave nearest me, and it was, "In evil memory of Julia Stone." And as usual Jack got up, and again I followed him through the hall and up the staircase with many corners. On this occasion it was darker than usual, and when I passed into the room in the tower I could only just see the furniture, the position of which was already familiar to me. Also there was a dreadful odour of decay in the room, and I woke screaming.

The dream, with such variations and developments as I have mentioned, went on at intervals for fifteen years. Sometimes I would dream it two or three nights in succession; once, as I have said, there was an intermission of six months, but taking a reasonable average, I should say that I dreamed it quite as often as once in a month. It had, as is plain, something of nightmare about it, since it always ended in the same appalling terror, which so far from getting less, seemed to me to gather fresh fear every time that I experienced it. There was, too, a strange and dreadful consistency about it. The characters in it, as I have mentioned, got regularly older, death and marriage visited this silent family, and I never in the dream, after Mrs. Stone had died, set eyes on her again. But it was always her voice that told me that the room in the tower was prepared for me, and whether we had tea out on the lawn, or the scene was laid in one of the rooms overlooking it, I could always see her gravestone standing just outside the iron gate. It was the same, too, with the married daughter; usually she was not present, but once or twice she returned again, in company with a man, whom I took to be her husband. He, too, like the rest of them, was always silent. But, owing to the constant repetition of the dream, I had ceased to attach, in my waking hours, any significance to it. I never met Jack Stone again during all those years, nor did I ever see a house that resembled this dark house of my dream. And then something happened.

I had been in London in this year, up till the end of July, and during the first week in August went down to stay with a friend in a house he had taken for the summer months, in the Ashdown Forest district of Sussex. I left London early, for John Clinton was to meet me at Forest Row Station, and we were going to spend the day golfing, and go to his house in the evening. He had his motor with him, and we set off, about five in the afternoon, after a thoroughly delightful day, for the drive, the distance being some ten miles. As it was still so early we did not have tea at the club house, but waited till we should get home. As we drove, the weather, which up till then had been, though hot, deliciously fresh, seemed to me to alter in quality, and become very stagnant and oppressive, and I felt that indefinable sense of ominous apprehension that I am accustomed to before thunder. John, however, did not share my views, attributing my loss of lightness to the fact that I had lost both my matches. Events proved, however, that I was right, though I do not think that the thunderstorm that broke that night was the sole cause of my depression.

Our way lay through deep high-banked lanes, and before we had gone very far I fell asleep, and was only awakened by the stopping of the motor. And with a sudden thrill, partly of fear but chiefly of curiosity, I found myself standing in the doorway of my house of dream. We went, I half wondering whether or not I was dreaming still, through a low oak-panelled hall, and out onto the lawn, where tea was laid in the shadow of the house. It was set in flower beds, a red-brick wall, with a gate in it, bounded one side, and out beyond that was a space of rough grass with a walnut tree. The façade of the house was very long, and at one end stood a three-storied tower, markedly older than the rest.

Here for the moment all resemblance to the repeated dream ceased. There was no silent and somehow terrible family, but a large assembly of exceedingly cheerful persons, all of whom were known to me. And in spite of the horror with which the dream itself had always filled me, I felt nothing of it now that the scene of it was thus reproduced before me. But I felt the intensest curiosity as to what was going to happen.

Tea pursued its cheerful course, and before long Mrs. Clinton got up. And at that moment I think I knew what she was going to say. She spoke to me, and what she said was:

"Jack will show you your room: I have given you the room in the tower."

At that, for half a second, the horror of the dream took hold of me again. But it quickly passed, and again I felt nothing more than the most intense curiosity. It was not very long before it was amply satisfied.

John turned to me.

"Right up at the top of the house," he said, "but I think you'll be comfortable. We're absolutely full up. Would you like to go and see it now? By Jove, I believe that you are right, and that we are going to have a thunderstorm. How dark it has become."

I got up and followed him. We passed through the hall, and up the perfectly familiar staircase. Then he opened the door, and I went in. And at that moment sheer unreasoning terror again possessed me. I did not know for certain what I feared: I simply feared. Then like a sudden recollection, when one remembers a name which has long escaped the memory, I knew what I feared. I feared Mrs. Stone, whose grave with the sinister inscription, "In evil memory," I had so often seen in my dream, just beyond the lawn which lay below my window. And then once more the fear passed so completely that I wondered what there was to fear, and I found myself, sober and quiet and sane, in the room in the tower, the name of which I had so often heard in my dream, and the scene of which was so familiar.

I looked around it with a certain sense of proprietorship, and found that nothing had been changed from the dreaming

nights in which I knew it so well. Just to the left of the door was
the bed, lengthways along the wall, with the head of it in the
angle. In a line with it was the fireplace and a small bookcase;
opposite the door the outer wall was pierced by two lattice-
paned windows, between which stood the dressing-table,
while ranged along the fourth wall was the washing-stand
and a big cupboard. My luggage had already been unpacked,
for the furniture of dressing and undressing lay orderly on
the wash-stand and toilet-table, while my dinner clothes
were spread out on the coverlet of the bed. And then, with a
sudden start of unexplained dismay, I saw that there were two
rather conspicuous objects which I had not seen before in my
dreams: one a life-sized oil painting of Mrs. Stone, the other a
black-and-white sketch of Jack Stone, representing him as he
had appeared to me only a week before in the last of the series
of these repeated dreams, a rather secret and evil-looking man
of about thirty. His picture hung between the windows, looking straight across the room to the other portrait, which hung
at the side of the bed. At that I looked next, and as I looked I
felt once more the horror of nightmare seize me.

It represented Mrs. Stone as I had seen her last in my
dreams: old and withered and white haired. But in spite of the
evident feebleness of body, a dreadful exuberance and vitality shone through the envelope of flesh, an exuberance wholly
malign, a vitality that foamed and frothed with unimagina-
ble evil. Evil beamed from the narrow, leering eyes; it laughed
in the demon-like mouth. The whole face was instinct with
some secret and appalling mirth; the hands, clasped together
on the knee, seemed shaking with suppressed and nameless
glee. Then I saw also that it was signed in the left-hand bottom
corner, and wondering who the artist could be, I looked more
closely, and read the inscription, "Julia Stone by Julia Stone."

There came a tap at the door, and John Clinton entered.

"Got everything you want?" he asked.

"Rather more than I want," said I, pointing to the picture. He laughed.

"Hard-featured old lady," he said. "By herself, too, I remember. Anyhow she can't have flattered herself much."

"But don't you see?" said I. "It's scarcely a human face at all. It's the face of some witch, of some devil."

He looked at it more closely.

"Yes; it isn't very pleasant," he said. "Scarcely a bedside manner, eh? Yes; I can imagine getting the nightmare, if I went to sleep with that close by my bed. I'll have it taken down if you like."

"I really wish you would," I said.

He rang the bell, and with the help of a servant we detached the picture and carried it out onto the landing, and put it with its face to the wall.

"By Jove, the old lady is a weight," said John, mopping his forehead. "I wonder if she had something on her mind."

The extraordinary weight of the picture had struck me too. I was about to reply, when I caught sight of my own hand. There was blood on it, in considerable quantities, covering the whole palm.

"I've cut myself somehow," said I.

John gave a little startled exclamation.

"Why, I have too," he said.

Simultaneously the footman took out his handkerchief and wiped his hand with it. I saw that there was blood also on his handkerchief.

John and I went back into the tower room and washed the blood off; but neither on his hand nor on mine was there the slightest trace of a scratch or cut. It seemed to me that, having ascertained this, we both, by a sort of tacit consent, did not allude to it again. Something in my case had dimly occurred to me that I did not wish to think about. It was but a conjecture, but I fancied that I knew the same thing had occurred to him.

The heat and oppression of the air, for the storm we had expected was still undischarged, increased very much after dinner, and for some time most of the party, among whom were John Clinton and myself, sat outside on the path bounding the lawn, where we had had tea. The night was absolutely dark, and no twinkle of star or moon ray could penetrate the pall of cloud that overset the sky. By degrees our assembly thinned, the women went up to bed, men dispersed to the smoking or billiard room, and by eleven o'clock my host and I were the only two left. All the evening I thought that he had something on his mind, and as soon as we were alone he spoke.

"The man who helped us with the picture had blood on his hand, too, did you notice?" he said. "I asked him just now if he had cut himself, and he said he supposed he had, but that he could find no mark of it. Now where did that blood come from?"

By dint of telling myself that I was not going to think about it, I had succeeded in not doing so, and I did not want, especially just at bedtime, to be reminded of it.

"I don't know," said I, "and I don't really care so long as the picture of Mrs. Julia Stone is not by my bed."

He got up.

"But it's odd," he said. "Ha! Now you'll see another odd thing."

A dog of his, an Irish terrier by breed, had come out of the house as we talked. The door behind us into the hall was open, and a bright oblong of light shone across the lawn to the iron gate which led on to the rough grass outside, where the walnut tree stood. I saw that the dog had all his hackles up, bristling with rage and fright; his lips were curled back from his teeth, as if he was ready to spring at something, and he was growling to himself. He took not the slightest notice of his master or me, but stiffly and tensely walked across the grass to the iron gate. There he stood for a moment, looking through the bars and still growling. Then of a sudden his courage seemed to desert him: he gave one long howl, and scuttled back to the house with a curious crouching sort of movement.

"He does that half-a-dozen times a day," said John. "He sees something which he both hates and fears."

I walked to the gate and looked over it. Something was moving on the grass outside, and soon a sound which I could not instantly identify came to my ears. Then I remembered what it was: it was the purring of a cat. I lit a match, and saw the purrer, a big blue Persian, walking round and round in a little circle just outside the gate, stepping high and ecstatically, with tail carried aloft like a banner. Its eyes were bright and shining, and every now and then it put its head down and sniffed at the grass.

I laughed.

"The end of that mystery, I am afraid." I said. "Here's a large cat having Walpurgis night all alone."

"Yes, that's Darius," said John. "He spends half the day and all night there. But that's not the end of the dog mystery, for Toby and he are the best of friends, but the beginning of the cat mystery. What's the cat doing there? And why is Darius pleased, while Toby is terror-stricken?"

At that moment I remembered the rather horrible detail of my dreams when I saw through the gate, just where the cat was now, the white tombstone with the sinister inscription. But before I could answer the rain began, as suddenly and heavily as if a tap had been turned on, and simultaneously the big cat squeezed through the bars of the gate, and came leaping across the lawn to the house for shelter. Then it sat in the doorway, looking out eagerly into the dark. It spat and struck at John with its paw, as he pushed it in, in order to close the door.

Somehow, with the portrait of Julia Stone in the passage outside, the room in the tower had absolutely no alarm for me, and as I went to bed, feeling very sleepy and heavy, I had nothing more than interest for the curious incident about our bleeding hands, and the conduct of the cat and dog. The last thing I looked at before I put out my light was the square empty space by my bed where the portrait had been. Here the paper was of its original full tint of dark red: over the rest of the walls it had faded. Then I blew out my candle and instantly fell asleep.

My awaking was equally instantaneous, and I sat bolt upright in bed under the impression that some bright light had been flashed in my face, though it was now absolutely pitch dark. I knew exactly where I was, in the room which I had dreaded in dreams, but no horror that I ever felt when asleep approached the fear that now invaded and froze my brain. Immediately after a peal of thunder crackled just above the house, but the probability that it was only a flash of lightning which awoke me gave no reassurance to my galloping heart. Something I knew was in the room with me, and instinctively I put out my right hand, which was nearest the wall, to keep it away. And my hand touched the edge of a picture-frame hanging close to me.

I sprang out of bed, upsetting the small table that stood by it, and I heard my watch, candle, and matches clatter onto the floor. But for the moment there was no need of light, for a blinding flash leaped out of the clouds, and showed me that by my bed again hung the picture of Mrs. Stone. And instantly the room went into blackness again. But in that flash I saw another thing also, namely a figure that leaned over the end of my bed, watching me. It was dressed in some close-clinging white garment, spotted and stained with mould, and the face was that of the portrait.

Overhead the thunder cracked and roared, and when it ceased and the deathly stillness succeeded, I heard the rustle of movement coming nearer me, and, more horrible yet, perceived an odour of corruption and decay. And then a hand was laid on the side of my neck, and close beside my ear I heard quick-taken, eager breathing. Yet I knew that this thing, though it could be perceived by touch, by smell, by eye and by ear, was still not of this earth, but something that had passed out of the body and had power to make itself manifest. Then a voice, already familiar to me, spoke.

"I knew you would come to the room in the tower," it said. "I have been long waiting for you. At last you have come. Tonight I shall feast; before long we will feast together."

And the quick breathing came closer to me; I could feel it on my neck.

At that the terror, which I think had paralysed me for the moment, gave way to the wild instinct of self-preservation. I hit wildly with both arms, kicking out at the same moment, and heard a little animal-squeal, and something soft dropped with a thud beside me. I took a couple of steps forward, nearly tripping up over whatever it was that lay there, and by the merest good-luck found the handle of the door. In another second I ran out on the landing, and had banged the door behind me. Almost at the same moment I heard a door open somewhere below, and John Clinton, candle in hand, came running upstairs.

"What is it?" he said. "I sleep just below you, and heard a noise as if—Good heavens, there's blood on your shoulder."

I stood there, so he told me afterwards, swaying from side to side, white as a sheet, with the mark on my shoulder as if a hand covered with blood had been laid there.

"It's in there," I said, pointing. "She, you know. The portrait is in there, too, hanging up on the place we took it from."

At that he laughed.

"My dear fellow, this is mere nightmare," he said.

He pushed by me, and opened the door, I standing there simply inert with terror, unable to stop him, unable to move.

"Phew! What an awful smell," he said.

Then there was silence; he had passed out of my sight behind the open door. Next moment he came out again, as white as myself, and instantly shut it.

"Yes, the portrait's there," he said, "and on the floor is a thing—a thing spotted with earth, like what they bury people in. Come away, quick, come away."

How I got downstairs I hardly know. An awful shuddering and nausea of the spirit rather than of the flesh had seized me, and more than once he had to place my feet upon the steps, while every now and then he cast glances of terror and apprehension up the stairs. But in time we came to his dressing-room on the floor below, and there I told him what I have here described.

*   *   *   *   *

The sequel can be made short; indeed, some of my readers have perhaps already guessed what it was, if they remember that inexplicable affair of the churchyard at West Fawley, some eight years ago, where an attempt was made three times to bury the body of a certain woman who had committed suicide. On each occasion the coffin was found in the course of a few days again protruding from the ground. After the third attempt, in order that the thing should not be talked about, the body was buried elsewhere in unconsecrated ground. Where it was buried was just outside the iron gate of the garden belonging to the house where this woman had lived. She had committed suicide in a room at the top of the tower in that house. Her name was Julia Stone.

Subsequently the body was again secretly dug up, and the coffin was found to be full of blood.

In the year 1913

13 Jan.	Various militias are organized into the Ulster Volunteer Force to resist Irish home rule.
9 Feb.	Mexican Revolution—beginning of the "Ten Tragic Days": coup d'état in Mexico City by opponents of President Francisco I. Madero.
23 Feb.	Joseph Stalin is arrested in Saint Petersburg by the Okhrana police and exiled to Siberia.
22 March	Song Jiaoren, Acting President of the Kuomintang Party, dies after being shot at Shanghai Railway Station two days earlier.
31 March	American banker J.P. Morgan dies in Rome, Italy, at the age of 75.
30 May	The First Balkan War ends with the signing of the Treaty of London.
4 June	British suffragette Emily Davison runs out in front of the King's horse, Anmer, at the Epsom Derby. She dies four days later.
29 June	The Second Balkan War begins when Bulgaria attacks Serbia and Greece.
10 Aug.	The Second Balkan War ends with the signing of the Treaty of Bucharest.
10 Oct.	Yuan Shikai is formally inaugurated as President of the Republic of China.
6 Nov.	Mohandas Gandhi is arrested for leading a march of Indian miners in South Africa.
12 Dec.	Art thief Vincenzo Peruggia is arrested when he tries to sell the *Mona Lisa* in Italy.
21 Dec.	The first crossword puzzle, created by Arthur Wynne, appears in the *New York World*.
23 Dec.	The Federal Reserve becomes the central banking system of the USA.

– 1913 –

The Horror of the Heights

Sir Arthur Conan Doyle

(WHICH INCLUDES THE MANUSCRIPT KNOWN AS THE JOYCE-ARMSTRONG FRAGMENT)

The idea that the extraordinary narrative which has been called the Joyce-Armstrong Fragment is an elaborate practical joke evolved by some unknown person, cursed by a perverted and sinister sense of humour, has now been abandoned by all who have examined the matter. The most *macabre* and imaginative of plotters would hesitate before linking his morbid fancies with the unquestioned and tragic facts which reinforce the statement. Though the assertions contained in it are amazing and even monstrous, it is none the less forcing itself upon the general intelligence that they are true, and that we must readjust our ideas to the new situation. This world of ours appears to be separated by a slight and precarious margin of safety from a most singular and unexpected danger. I will endeavour in this narrative, which reproduces the original document in its necessarily somewhat fragmentary form, to lay before the reader the whole of the facts up to date, prefacing my statement by saying that, if there be any who doubt the narrative of Joyce-Armstrong, there can be no question at all as to the facts concerning Lieutenant Myrtle, R. N., and Mr. Hay Connor, who undoubtedly met their end in the manner described.

The Joyce-Armstrong Fragment was found in the field which is called Lower Haycock, lying one mile to the westward of the village of Withyham, upon the Kent and Sussex border. It was on the fifteenth of September last that an agricultural labourer, James Flynn, in the employment of Mathew Dodd, farmer, of the Chauntry Farm, Withyham, perceived a briar pipe lying near the footpath which skirts the hedge in Lower Haycock. A few paces farther on he picked up a pair of broken binocular glasses. Finally, among some nettles in the ditch, he caught sight of a flat, canvas-backed book, which proved to be a note-book with detachable leaves, some of which had come loose and were fluttering along the base of the hedge. These he collected, but some, including the first, were never recovered, and leave a deplorable hiatus in this all-important statement. The note-book was taken by the labourer to his master, who in turn showed it to Dr. J. H. Atherton, of Hartfield. This gentleman at once recognized the need for an expert examination, and the manuscript was forwarded to the Aero Club in London, where it now lies.

The first two pages of the manuscript are missing. There is also one torn away at the end of the narrative, though none of these affect the general coherence of the story. It is conjectured that the missing opening is concerned with the record of Mr. Joyce-Armstrong's qualifications as an aeronaut, which can be gathered from other sources and are admitted to be unsurpassed among the air-pilots of England. For many years he has been looked upon as among the most daring and the most intellectual of flying men, a combination which has enabled him to both invent and test several new devices, including the common gyroscopic attachment which is known by his name. The main body of the manuscript is written neatly in ink, but the last few lines are in pencil and are so ragged as to be hardly legible—exactly, in fact, as they might be expected to appear if they were scribbled off hurriedly from the seat of a moving aeroplane. There are, it may be added, several stains, both on the last page and on the outside cover, which have been pronounced by the Home Office experts to be blood—probably human and certainly mammalian. The fact that something closely resembling the organism of malaria was discovered in this blood, and that Joyce-Armstrong is known to have suffered from intermittent fever, is a remarkable example of the new weapons which modern science has placed in the hands of our detectives.

And now a word as to the personality of the author of this epoch-making statement. Joyce-Armstrong, according to the few friends who really knew something of the man, was a poet and a dreamer, as well as a mechanic and an inventor. He was a man of considerable wealth, much of which he had spent in the pursuit of his aeronautical hobby. He had four private aeroplanes in his hangars near Devizes, and is said to have made no fewer than one hundred and seventy ascents in the course of last year. He was a retiring man with dark moods, in which he would avoid the society of his fellows. Captain Dangerfield, who knew him better than anyone, says that there were times when his eccentricity threatened to develop into something more serious. His habit of carrying a shot-gun with him in his aeroplane was one manifestation of it.

Another was the morbid effect which the fall of Lieutenant Myrtle had upon his mind. Myrtle, who was attempting the height record, fell from an altitude of something over thirty thousand feet. Horrible to narrate, his head was entirely obliterated, though his body and limbs preserved their configuration. At every gathering of airmen, Joyce-Armstrong, according to Dangerfield, would ask, with an enigmatic smile: "And where, pray, is Myrtle's head?"

On another occasion after dinner, at the mess of the Flying School on Salisbury Plain, he started a debate as to what will be the most permanent danger which airmen will have to encounter. Having listened to successive opinions as to air-pockets, faulty construction, and over-banking, he ended by shrugging his shoulders and refusing to put forward his own views, though he gave the impression that they differed from any advanced by his companions.

It is worth remarking that after his own complete disappearance it was found that his private affairs were arranged with a precision which may show that he had a strong premonition of disaster. With these essential explanations I will now give the narrative exactly as it stands, beginning at page three of the blood-soaked note-book:—

"Nevertheless, when I dined at Rheims with Coselli and Gustav Raymond I found that neither of them was aware of any particular danger in the higher layers of the atmosphere. I did not actually say what was in my thoughts, but I got so near to it that if they had any corresponding idea they could not have failed to express it. But then they are two empty, vainglorious fellows with no thought beyond seeing their silly names in the newspaper. It is interesting to note that neither of them had ever been much beyond the twenty-thousand-foot level. Of course, men have been higher than this both in balloons and in the ascent of mountains. It must be well above that point that the aeroplane enters the danger zone—always presuming that my premonitions are correct.

"Aeroplaning has been with us now for more than twenty years, and one might well ask: Why should this peril be only revealing itself in our day? The answer is obvious. In the old days of weak engines, when a hundred horse-power Gnome or Green was considered ample for every need, the flights were very restricted. Now that three hundred horse-power is the rule rather than the exception, visits to the upper layers have become easier and more common. Some of us can remember how, in our youth, Garros made a world-wide reputation by attaining nineteen thousand feet, and it was considered a remarkable achievement to fly over the Alps. Our standard now has been immeasurably raised, and there are twenty high flights for one in former years. Many of them have been undertaken with impunity. The thirty-thousand-foot level has been reached time after time with no discomfort beyond cold and asthma. What does this prove? A visitor might descend upon this planet a thousand times and never see a tiger. Yet tigers exist, and if he chanced to come down into a jungle he might be devoured. There are jungles of the upper air, and there are worse things than tigers which inhabit them. I believe in time they will map these jungles accurately out. Even at the present moment I could name two of them. One of them lies over the Pau-Biarritz district of France. Another is just over my head as I write here in my house in Wiltshire. I rather think there is a third in the Homburg-Wiesbaden district.

"It was the disappearance of the airmen that first set me thinking. Of course, everyone said that they had fallen into the sea, but that did not satisfy me at all. First, there was Verrier in France; his machine was found near Bayonne, but they never got his body. There was the case of Baxter also, who vanished, though his engine and some of the iron fixings were found in a wood in Leicestershire. In that case, Dr. Middleton, of Amesbury, who was watching the flight with a telescope, declares that just before the clouds obscured the view he saw the machine, which was at an enormous height, suddenly rise perpendicularly upwards in a succession of jerks in a manner that he would have thought to be impossible. That was the last seen of Baxter. There was a correspondence in the papers, but it never led to anything. There were several other similar cases, and then there was the death of Hay Connor. What a cackle there was about an unsolved mystery of the air, and what columns in the halfpenny papers, and yet how little was ever done to get to the bottom of the business! He came down in a tremendous vol-plané[1] from an unknown height. He never got off his machine and died in his pilot's seat. Died of what? 'Heart disease,' said the doctors. Rubbish! Hay Connor's heart was as sound as mine is. What did Venables say? Venables was the only man who was at his side when he died. He said that he was shivering and looked like a man who had been badly scared. 'Died of fright,' said Venables, but could not imagine what he was frightened about. Only said one word to Venables, which sounded like 'Monstrous.' They could make nothing of that at the inquest. But I could make something of it. Monsters! That was the last word of poor Harry Hay Connor. And he *did* die of fright, just as Venables thought.

"And then there was Myrtle's head. Do you really believe—does anybody really believe—that a man's head could be driven clean into his body by the force of a fall? Well, perhaps it may be possible, but I, for one, have never believed that it was so with Myrtle. And the grease upon his clothes—'all slimy with grease,' said somebody at the inquest. Queer that nobody got thinking after that! I did—but, then, I had been thinking for a good long time. I've made three ascents—how Dangerfield used to chaff me about my shot-gun!—but I've never been high enough. Now, with this new light Paul Veroner machine and its one hundred and seventy-five Robur, I should easily touch the thirty thousand tomorrow. I'll have a shot at the record. Maybe I shall have a shot at something else as well. Of course, it's dangerous. If a fellow wants to avoid danger he had best keep out of flying altogether and subside finally into flannel slippers and a dressing-gown. But I'll visit the air-jungle tomorrow—and if there's anything there I shall know it. If I return, I'll find myself a bit of a celebrity. If I don't, this note-book may explain what I am trying to do, and how I lost my life in doing it. But no drivel about accidents or mysteries, if *you* please.

---

1   To glide towards the ground with no engine power.

"I chose my Paul Veroner monoplane for the job. There's nothing like a monoplane when real work is to be done. Beaumont[2] found that out in very early days. For one thing, it doesn't mind damp, and the weather looks as if we should be in the clouds all the time. It's a bonny little model and answers my hand like a tender-mouthed horse. The engine is a ten-cylinder rotary Robur working up to one hundred and seventy-five. It has all the modern improvements—enclosed fuselage, high-curved landing skids, brakes, gyroscopic steadiers, and three speeds, worked by an alteration of the angle of the planes upon the Venetian-blind principle. I took a shotgun with me and a dozen cartridges filled with buck-shot. You should have seen the face of Perkins, my old mechanic, when I directed him to put them in. I was dressed like an Arctic explorer, with two jerseys under my overalls, thick socks inside my padded boots, a storm-cap with flaps, and my talc goggles. It was stifling outside the hangars, but I was going for the summit of the Himalayas, and had to dress for the part. Perkins knew there was something on and implored me to take him with me. Perhaps I should if I were using the biplane, but a monoplane is a one-man show—if you want to get the last foot of lift out of it. Of course, I took an oxygen bag; the man who goes for the altitude record without one will either be frozen or smothered—or both.

"I had a good look at the planes, the rudder-bar, and the elevating lever before I got in. Everything was in order so far as I could see. Then I switched on my engine and found that she was running sweetly. When they let her go she rose almost at once upon the lowest speed. I circled my home field once or twice just to warm her up, and then, with a wave to Perkins and the others, I flattened out my planes and put her on her highest.

---

2   Most likely a reference to André Beaumont, pseudonym of the French aviator and Naval Lieutenant Jean Louis Conneau (1880–1937).

She skimmed like a swallow down wind for eight or ten miles until I turned her nose up a little and she began to climb in a great spiral for the cloud-bank above me. It's all-important to rise slowly and adapt yourself to the pressure as you go.

"It was a close, warm day for an English September, and there was the hush and heaviness of impending rain. Now and then there came sudden puffs of wind from the south-west—one of them so gusty and unexpected that it caught me napping and turned me half-round for an instant. I remember the time when gusts and whirls and air-pockets used to be things of danger—before we learned to put an over-mastering power into our engines. Just as I reached the cloud-banks, with the altimeter marking three thousand, down came the rain. My word, how it poured! It drummed upon my wings and lashed against my face, blurring my glasses so that I could hardly see. I got down on to a low speed, for it was painful to travel against it. As I got higher it became hail, and I had to turn tail to it. One of my cylinders was out of action—a dirty plug, I should imagine, but still I was rising steadily with plenty of power. After a bit the trouble passed, whatever it was, and I heard the full, deep-throated purr—the ten singing as one. That's where the beauty of our modern silencers comes in. We can at last control our engines by ear. How they squeal and squeak and sob when they are in trouble! All those cries for help were wasted in the old days, when every sound was swallowed up by the monstrous racket of the machine. If only the early aviators could come back to see the beauty and per-fection of the mechanism which have been bought at the cost of their lives!

"About nine-thirty I was nearing the clouds. Down below me, all blurred and shadowed with rain, lay the vast expanse of Salisbury Plain. Half-a-dozen flying machines were doing hack-work at the thousand-foot level, looking like little black swallows against the green background. I dare say they were wondering what I was doing up in cloud-land. Suddenly a grey curtain drew across beneath me and the wet folds of vapour were swirling round my face. It was clammily cold and miserable. But I was above the hail-storm, and that was something gained. The cloud was as dark and thick as a London fog. In my anxiety to get clear, I cocked her nose up until the automatic alarm-bell rang, and I actually began to slide backwards. My sopped and dripping wings had made me heavier than I thought, but presently I was in lighter cloud, and soon had cleared the first layer. There was a second—opal-coloured and fleecy—at a great height above my head, a white unbroken ceiling above, and a dark unbroken floor below, with the monoplane labouring upwards upon a vast spiral between them. It is deadly lonely in these cloud-spaces. Once a great flight of some small water-birds went past me, flying very fast to the westwards. The quick whirr of their wings and their musical cry were cheery to my ear. I fancy that they were teal, but I am a wretched zoologist. Now that we humans have become birds we must really learn to know our brethren by sight.

"The wind down beneath me whirled and swayed the broad cloud-plain. Once a great eddy formed in it, a whirlpool of vapour, and through it, as down a funnel, I caught sight of the distant world. A large white biplane was passing at a vast depth beneath me. I fancy it was the morning mail service betwixt Bristol and London. Then the drift swirled inwards again and the great solitude was unbroken.

"Just after ten I touched the lower edge of the upper cloud-stratum. It consisted of fine diaphanous vapour drifting swiftly from the westward. The wind had been steadily rising all this time and it was now blowing a sharp breeze—twenty-eight an hour by my gauge. Already it was very cold, though my altimeter only marked nine thousand. The engines were working beautifully, and we went droning steadily upwards.

The cloud-bank was thicker than I had expected, but at last it thinned out into a golden mist before me, and then in an instant I had shot out from it, and there was an unclouded sky and a brilliant sun above my head—all blue and gold above, all shining silver below, one vast glimmering plain as far as my eyes could reach. It was a quarter past ten o'clock, and the barograph needle pointed to twelve thousand eight hundred. Up I went and up, my ears concentrated upon the deep purring of my motor, my eyes busy always with the watch, the revolution indicator, the petrol lever, and the oil pump. No wonder aviators are said to be a fearless race. With so many things to think of there is no time to trouble about oneself. About this time I noted how unreliable is the compass when above a certain height from earth. At fifteen thousand feet mine was pointing east and a point south. The sun and the wind gave me my true bearings.

"I had hoped to reach an eternal stillness in these high altitudes, but with every thousand feet of ascent the gale grew stronger. My machine groaned and trembled in every joint and rivet as she faced it, and swept away like a sheet of paper when I banked her on the turn, skimming down wind at a greater pace, perhaps, than ever mortal man has moved. Yet I had always to turn again and tack up in the wind's eye, for it was not merely a height record that I was after. By all my calculations it was above little Wiltshire that my air-jungle lay, and all my labour might be lost if I struck the outer layers at some farther point.

"When I reached the nineteen-thousand-foot level, which was about midday, the wind was so severe that I looked with some anxiety to the stays of my wings, expecting momentarily to see them snap or slacken. I even cast loose the parachute behind me, and fastened its hook into the ring of my leathern belt, so as to be ready for the worst. Now was the time when a bit of scamped work by the mechanic is paid for by the life of the aeronaut. But she held together bravely. Every cord and strut was humming and vibrating like so many harp-strings, but it was glorious to see how, for all the beating and the buffeting, she was still the conqueror of Nature and the mistress of the sky. There is surely something divine in man himself that he should rise so superior to the limitations which Creation seemed to impose—rise, too, by such unselfish, heroic devotion as this air-conquest has shown. Talk of human degeneration! When has such a story as this been written in the annals of our race?

"These were the thoughts in my head as I climbed that monstrous inclined plane with the wind sometimes beating in my face and sometimes whistling behind my ears, while the cloud-land beneath me fell away to such a distance that the folds and hummocks of silver had all smoothed out into one flat, shining plain. But suddenly I had a horrible and unprecedented experience. I have known before what it is to be in what our neighbours have called a *tourbillon*,[3] but never on such a scale as this. That huge, sweeping river of wind of which I have spoken had, as it appears, whirlpools within it which were as monstrous as itself. Without a moment's warning I was dragged suddenly into the heart of one. I spun round for a minute or two with such velocity that I almost lost my senses, and then fell suddenly, left wing foremost, down the vacuum funnel in the centre. I dropped like a stone, and lost nearly a thousand feet. It was only my belt that kept me in my seat, and the shock and breathlessness left me hanging half-insensible over the side of the fuselage. But I am always capable of a supreme effort—it is my one great merit as an aviator. I was conscious that the descent was slower. The whirlpool was a cone rather than a funnel, and I had come to the apex. With a terrific wrench, throwing my weight all to

---

3 Whirlwind.

one side, I levelled my planes and brought her head away from the wind. In an instant I had shot out of the eddies and was skimming down the sky. Then, shaken but victorious, I turned her nose up and began once more my steady grind on the upward spiral. I took a large sweep to avoid the danger-spot of the whirlpool, and soon I was safely above it. Just after one o'clock I was twenty-one thousand feet above the sea-level. To my great joy I had topped the gale, and with every hundred feet of ascent the air grew stiller. On the other hand, it was very cold, and I was conscious of that peculiar nausea which goes with rarefaction of the air. For the first time I unscrewed the mouth of my oxygen bag and took an occasional whiff of the glorious gas. I could feel it running like a cordial through my veins, and I was exhilarated almost to the point of drunkenness. I shouted and sang as I soared upwards into the cold, still outer world.

"It is very clear to me that the insensibility which came upon Glaisher, and in a lesser degree upon Coxwell, when, in 1862, they ascended in a balloon to the height of thirty thousand feet, was due to the extreme speed with which a perpendicular ascent is made. Doing it at an easy gradient and accustoming oneself to the lessened barometric pressure by slow degrees, there are no such dreadful symptoms. At the same great height I found that even without my oxygen inhaler I could breathe without undue distress. It was bitterly cold, however, and my thermometer was at zero Fahrenheit. At one-thirty I was nearly seven miles above the surface of the earth, and still ascending steadily. I found, however, that the rarefied air was giving markedly less support to my planes, and that my angle of ascent had to be considerably lowered in consequence. It was already clear that even with my light weight and strong engine-power there was a point in front of me where I should be held. To make matters worse, one of my sparking-plugs was in trouble again and there was intermittent misfiring in the engine. My heart was heavy with the fear of failure.

"It was about that time that I had a most extraordinary experience. Something whizzed past me in a trail of smoke and exploded with a loud, hissing sound, sending forth a cloud of steam. For the instant I could not imagine what had happened. Then I remembered that the earth is for ever being bombarded by meteor stones, and would be hardly inhabitable were they not in nearly every case turned to vapour in the outer layers of the atmosphere. Here is a new danger for the high-altitude man, for two others passed me when I was nearing the forty-thousand-foot mark. I cannot doubt that at the edge of the earth's envelope the risk would be a very real one.

"My barograph needle marked forty-one thousand three hundred when I became aware that I could go no farther. Physically, the strain was not as yet greater than I could bear, but my machine had reached its limit. The attenuated air gave no firm support to the wings, and the least tilt developed into side-slip, while she seemed sluggish on her controls. Possibly, had the engine been at its best, another thousand feet might have been within our capacity, but it was still misfiring, and two out of the ten cylinders appeared to be out of action. If I had not already reached the zone for which I was searching then I should never see it upon this journey. But was it not possible that I had attained it? Soaring in circles like a monstrous hawk upon the forty-thousand-foot level I let the monoplane guide herself, and with my Mannheim glass I made a careful observation of my surroundings. The heavens were perfectly clear; there was no indication of those dangers which I had imagined.

"I have said that I was soaring in circles. It struck me suddenly that I would do well to take a wider sweep and open up a new air-tract. If the hunter entered an earth-jungle he would drive through it if he wished to find his game. My reasoning had led me to believe that the air-jungle which I had imagined lay somewhere over Wiltshire. This should be to the south and west of me. I took my bearings from the sun, for the compass was hopeless and no trace of earth was to be seen—nothing but the distant, silver cloud-plain. However, I got my direction as best I might and kept her head straight to the mark. I reckoned that my petrol supply would not last for more than another hour or so, but I could afford to use it to the last drop, since a single magnificent vol-plané could at any time take me to the earth.

"Suddenly I was aware of something new. The air in front of me had lost its crystal clearness. It was full of long, ragged wisps of something which I can only compare to very fine cigarette smoke. It hung about in wreaths and coils, turning and twisting slowly in the sunlight. As the monoplane shot through it, I was aware of a faint taste of oil upon my lips, and there was a greasy scum upon the woodwork of the machine. Some infinitely fine organic matter appeared to be suspended in the atmosphere. There was no life there. It was inchoate and diffuse, extending for many square acres and then fringing off into the void. No, it was not life. But might it not be the remains of life? Above all, might it not be the food of life, of monstrous life, even as the humble grease of the ocean is the food for the mighty whale? The thought was in my mind when my eyes looked upwards and I saw the most wonderful vision that ever man has seen. Can I hope to convey it to you even as I saw it myself last Thursday?

"Conceive a jelly-fish such as sails in our summer seas, bell-shaped and of enormous size—far larger, I should judge, than the dome of St. Paul's. It was of a light pink colour veined with a delicate green, but the whole huge fabric so tenuous that it was but a fairy outline against the dark blue sky. It pulsated with a delicate and regular rhythm. From it there depended two long, drooping, green tentacles, which swayed slowly backwards and forwards. This gorgeous vision passed gently with noiseless dignity over my head, as light and fragile as a soap-bubble, and drifted upon its stately way.

"I had half-turned my monoplane, that I might look after this beautiful creature, when, in a moment, I found myself amidst a perfect fleet of them, of all sizes, but none so large as the first. Some were quite small, but the majority about as big as an average balloon, and with much the same curvature at the top. There was in them a delicacy of texture and colouring which reminded me of the finest Venetian glass. Pale shades of pink and green were the prevailing tints, but all had a lovely iridescence where the sun shimmered through their dainty forms. Some hundreds of them drifted past me, a wonderful fairy squadron of strange, unknown argosies of the sky—creatures whose forms and substance were so attuned to these pure heights that one could not conceive anything so delicate within actual sight or sound of earth.

"But soon my attention was drawn to a new phenomenon—the serpents of the outer air. These were long, thin, fantastic coils of vapour-like material, which turned and twisted with great speed, flying round and round at such a pace that the eyes could hardly follow them. Some of these ghost-like creatures were twenty or thirty feet long, but it was difficult to tell their girth, for their outline was so hazy that it seemed to fade away into the air around them. These air-snakes were of a very light grey or smoke colour, with some darker lines within, which gave the impression of a definite organism. One of them whisked past my very face, and I was conscious of a cold, clammy contact, but their composition was so unsubstantial that I could not connect them with any thought of physical danger, any more than the beautiful bell-like creatures which had preceded them. There was no more solidity in their frames than in the floating spume from a broken wave.

"But a more terrible experience was in store for me. Floating downwards from a great height there came a purplish patch of vapour, small as I saw it first, but rapidly enlarging as it approached me, until it appeared to be hundreds of square feet in size. Though fashioned of some transparent, jelly-like substance, it was none the less of much more definite outline and solid consistence than anything which I had seen before. There were more traces, too, of a physical organization, especially two vast, shadowy, circular plates upon either side, which may have been eyes, and a perfectly solid white projection between them which was as curved and cruel as the beak of a vulture.

"The whole aspect of this monster was formidable and threatening, and it kept changing its colour from a very light mauve to a dark, angry purple so thick that it cast a shadow as it drifted between my monoplane and the sun. On the upper curve of its huge body there were three great projections which I can only describe as enormous bubbles, and I was convinced as I looked at them that they were charged with some extremely light gas which served to buoy up the misshapen and semi-solid mass in the rarefied air. The creature moved swiftly along, keeping pace easily with the monoplane, and for twenty miles or more it formed my horrible escort, hovering over me like a bird of prey which is waiting to pounce. Its method of progression—done so swiftly that it was not easy to follow—was to throw out a long, glutinous streamer in front of it, which in turn seemed to draw forward the rest of the writhing body. So elastic and gelatinous was it that never for two successive minutes was it the same shape, and yet each change made it more threatening and loathsome than the last.

"I knew that it meant mischief. Every purple flush of its hideous body told me so. The vague, goggling eyes which were turned always upon me were cold and merciless in their viscid

From it there depended two long, drooping, green tentacles,
which swayed slowly backwards and forwards.

hatred. I dipped the nose of my monoplane downwards to escape it. As I did so, as quick as a flash there shot out a long tentacle from this mass of floating blubber, and it fell as light and sinuous as a whip-lash across the front of my machine. There was a loud hiss as it lay for a moment across the hot engine, and it whisked itself into the air again, while the huge, flat body drew itself together as if in sudden pain. I dipped to a vol-piqué,[4] but again a tentacle fell over the monoplane and was shorn off by the propeller as easily as it might have cut through a smoke wreath. A long, gliding, sticky, serpent-like coil came from behind and caught me round the waist, dragging me out of the fuselage. I tore at it, my fingers sinking into the smooth, glue-like surface, and for an instant I disengaged myself, but only to be caught round the boot by another coil, which gave me a jerk that tilted me almost on to my back.

"As I fell over I blazed off both barrels of my gun, though, indeed, it was like attacking an elephant with a pea-shooter to imagine that any human weapon could cripple that mighty bulk. And yet I aimed better than I knew, for, with a loud report, one of the great blisters upon the creature's back exploded with the puncture of the buck-shot. It was very clear that my conjecture was right, and that these vast clear bladders were distended with some lifting gas, for in an instant the huge cloud-like body turned sideways, writhing desperately to find its balance, while the white beak snapped and gaped in horrible fury. But already I had shot away on the steepest glide that I dared to attempt, my engine still full on, the flying propeller and the force of gravity shooting me downwards like an aerolite.[5] Far behind me I saw a dull, purplish smudge growing swiftly smaller and merging into the blue sky behind it. I was safe out of the deadly jungle of the outer air.

---

4   Nose dive.

5   A stony meteorite.

"Once out of danger I throttled my engine, for nothing tears a machine to pieces quicker than running on full power from a height. It was a glorious spiral vol-plané from nearly eight miles of altitude—first, to the level of the silver cloud-bank, then to that of the storm-cloud beneath it, and finally, in beating rain, to the surface of the earth. I saw the Bristol Channel beneath me as I broke from the clouds, but, having still some petrol in my tank, I got twenty miles inland before I found myself stranded in a field half a mile from the village of Ashcombe. There I got three tins of petrol from a passing motor-car, and at ten minutes past six that evening I alighted gently in my own home meadow at Devizes, after such a journey as no mortal upon earth has ever yet taken and lived to tell the tale. I have seen the beauty and I have seen the horror of the heights—and greater beauty or greater horror than that is not within the ken of man.

"And now it is my plan to go once again before I give my results to the world. My reason for this is that I must surely have something to show by way of proof before I lay such a tale before my fellow-men. It is true that others will soon follow and will confirm what I have said, and yet I should wish to carry conviction from the first. Those lovely iridescent bubbles of the air should not be hard to capture. They drift slowly upon their way, and the swift monoplane could intercept their leisurely course. It is likely enough that they would dissolve in the heavier layers of the atmosphere, and that some small heap of amorphous jelly might be all that I should bring to earth with me. And yet something there would surely be by which I could substantiate my story. Yes, I will go, even if I run a risk by doing so. These purple horrors would not seem to be numerous. It is probable that I shall not see one. If I do I shall dive at once. At the worst there is always the shot-gun and my knowledge of …"

Here a page of the manuscript is unfortunately missing. On the next page is written, in large, straggling writing:—

"Forty-three thousand feet. I shall never see earth again. They are beneath me, three of them. God help me; it is a dreadful death to die!"

Such in its entirety is the Joyce-Armstrong Statement. Of the man nothing has since been seen. Pieces of his shattered monoplane have been picked up in the preserves of Mr. Budd-Lushington upon the borders of Kent and Sussex, within a few miles of the spot where the note-book was discovered. If the unfortunate aviator's theory is correct that this air-jungle, as he called it, existed only over the south-west of England, then it would seem that he had fled from it at the full speed of his monoplane, but had been overtaken and devoured by these horrible creatures at some spot in the outer atmosphere above the place where the grim relics were found. The picture of that monoplane skimming down the sky, with the nameless terrors flying as swiftly beneath it and cutting it off always from the earth while they gradually closed in upon their victim, is one upon which a man who valued his sanity would prefer not to dwell. There are many, as I am aware, who still jeer at the facts which I have here set down, but even they must admit that Joyce-Armstrong has disappeared, and I would commend to them his own words: "This note-book may explain what I am trying to do, and how I lost my life in doing it. But no drivel about accidents or mysteries, if *you* please."

In the year 1914

21 April	The USA begins a seven-month occupation of Veracruz, Mexico.
28 June	Archduke Franz Ferdinand of Austria, and his wife, Sophie, Duchess of Hohenberg, are assassinated by Bosnian Serb Gavrilo Princip in Sarajevo.
28 July	Beginning of World War I: the Austro-Hungarian Empire declares war on Serbia.
1 Aug.	Germany declares war on Russia, following Russia's mobilisation in support of Serbia.
2 Aug.	Germany invades Luxembourg.
4 Aug.	Germany invades Belgium. Britain declares war on Germany.
15 Aug.	The Panama Canal opens to traffic, with the SS *Ancon* making the first official transit.
23 Aug.	The Battle of Mons takes place in Belgium. The British are forced to retreat.
5 Sept.	The First Battle of the Marne begins in France. The German advance is pushed back.
18 Sept.	The Government of Ireland Act 1914 (the Home Rule Act) receives royal assent.
19 Oct.	The First Battle of Ypres begins in West Flanders, Belgium.
29 Oct.	Ottoman warships shell Russian Black Sea ports; Russia, France, and Britain subsequently declare war on the Ottoman Empire in early November.
7 Nov.	Siege of Tsingtao: the German garrison in Tsingtao (Qingdao), China, surrenders to Japanese and British forces.
24–25 Dec.	The Christmas truce: a series of unofficial cease-fires occur along the Western Front.

— 1914 —

Dracula's Guest

Bram Stoker

When we started for our drive the sun was shining brightly on Munich, and the air was full of the joyousness of early summer. Just as we were about to depart, Herr Delbrück (the maître d'hôtel of the Quatre Saisons, where I was staying) came down, bareheaded, to the carriage and, after wishing me a pleasant drive, said to the coachman, still holding his hand on the handle of the carriage door:

"Remember you are back by nightfall. The sky looks bright but there is a shiver in the north wind that says there may be a sudden storm. But I am sure you will not be late." Here he smiled, and added "for you know what night it is."

Johann answered with an emphatic, "Ja, mein Herr," and, touching his hat, drove off quickly. When we had cleared the town, I said, after signalling to him to stop:

"Tell me, Johann, what is tonight?"

He crossed himself, as he answered laconically: "Walpurgis-nacht." Then he took out his watch, a great, old-fashioned German silver thing as big as a turnip and looked at it, with his eyebrows gathered together and a little impatient shrug of his shoulders. I realized that this was his way of respectfully protesting against the unnecessary delay, and sank back in the carriage, merely motioning him to proceed. He started off rapidly, as if to make up for lost time. Every now and then the horses seemed to throw up their heads and sniff the air suspiciously. On such occasions I often looked round in alarm. The road was pretty bleak, for we were traversing a sort of high, windswept plateau. As we drove, I saw a road that looked but little used and which seemed to dip through a little, winding valley. It looked so inviting that, even at the risk of offending him, I called Johann to stop—and when he had pulled up, I told him I would like to drive down that road. He made all sorts of excuses, and frequently crossed himself as he spoke. This somewhat piqued my curiosity, so I asked him various questions. He answered fencingly, and repeatedly looked at his watch in protest. Finally I said:

"Well, Johann, I want to go down this road. I shall not ask you to come unless you like; but tell me why you do not like to go, that is all I ask." For answer he seemed to throw himself off the box, so quickly did he reach the ground. Then he stretched out his hands appealingly to me, and implored me not to go. There was just enough of English mixed with the German for me to understand the drift of his talk. He seemed always just about to tell me something—the very idea of which evidently frightened him; but each time he pulled himself up saying, as he crossed himself: "Walpurgis-nacht!"

I tried to argue with him, but it was difficult to argue with a man when I did not know his language. The advantage certainly rested with him, for although he began to speak in English, of a very crude and broken kind, he always got excited and broke into his native tongue—and every time he did so, he looked at his watch. Then the horses became restless and sniffed the air. At this he grew very pale, and, looking around in a frightened way, he suddenly jumped forward, took them by the bridles and led them on some twenty feet. I followed, and asked why he had done this. For answer he crossed himself, pointed to the spot we had left and drew his carriage in the direction of the other road, indicating a cross, and said, first in German, then in English: "Buried him—him what killed themselves."

I remembered the old custom of burying suicides at cross-roads: "Ah! I see, a suicide. How interesting!" But for the life of me I could not make out why the horses were frightened.

Whilst we were talking, we heard a sort of sound between a yelp and a bark. It was far away; but the horses got very restless, and it took Johann all his time to quiet them. He was pale, and said: "It sounds like a wolf—but yet there are no wolves here now."

"No?" I said, questioning him; "isn't it long since the wolves were so near the city?"

"Long, long," he answered, "in the spring and summer; but with the snow the wolves have been here not so long."

Whilst he was petting the horses and trying to quiet them, dark clouds drifted rapidly across the sky. The sunshine passed away, and a breath of cold wind seemed to drift past us. It was only a breath, however, and more of a warning than a fact, for the sun came out brightly again. Johann looked under his lifted hand at the horizon and said:

"The storm of snow, he comes before long time."

Then he looked at his watch again, and, straightway holding his reins firmly—for the horses were still pawing the ground restlessly and shaking their heads—he climbed to his box as though the time had come for proceeding on our journey.

I felt a little obstinate and did not at once get into the carriage.

"Tell me," I said, "about this place where the road leads," and I pointed down.

Again he crossed himself and mumbled a prayer, before he answered: "It is unholy."

"What is unholy?" I enquired.

"The village."

"Then there is a village?"

"No, no. No one lives there hundreds of years."

My curiosity was piqued: "But you said there was a village."

"There was."

"Where is it now?"

Whereupon he burst out into a long story in German and English, so mixed up that I could not quite understand exactly what he said, but roughly I gathered that long ago, hundreds of years, men had died there and been buried in their graves; and sounds were heard under the clay, and when the graves were opened, men and women were found rosy with life, and their mouths red with blood. And so, in haste to save their lives (aye, and their souls!—and here he crossed himself) those who were left fled away to other places, where the living lived, and the dead were dead and not—not something. He was evidently afraid to speak the last words. As he proceeded with his narration, he grew more and more excited. It seemed as if his imagination had got hold of him, and he ended in a perfect paroxysm of fear—white-faced, perspiring, trembling and looking round him, as if expecting that some dreadful presence would manifest itself there in the bright sunshine on the open plain. Finally, in an agony of desperation, he cried:

"Walpurgis-nacht!" and pointed to the carriage for me to get in. All my English blood rose at this, and, standing back, I said:

"You are afraid, Johann—you are afraid. Go home; I shall return alone; the walk will do me good." The carriage door was open. I took from the seat my oak walking-stick—which I always carry on my holiday excursions—and closed the door, pointing back to Munich, and said, "Go home, Johann—Walpurgis-nacht doesn't concern Englishmen."

The horses were now more restive than ever, and Johann was trying to hold them in, while excitedly imploring me not to do anything so foolish. I pitied the poor fellow, he was so deeply in earnest; but all the same I could not help laughing.

His English was quite gone now. In his anxiety he had for-gotten that his only means of making me understand was to talk my language, so he jabbered away in his native German. It began to be a little tedious. After giving the direction, "Home!" I turned to go down the cross-road into the valley.

With a despairing gesture, Johann turned his horses towards Munich. I leaned on my stick and looked after him. He went slowly along the road for a while: then there came over the crest of the hill a man tall and thin. I could see so much in the distance. When he drew near the horses, they began to jump and kick about, then to scream with terror. Johann could not hold them in; they bolted down the road, running away madly. I watched them out of sight, then looked for the stranger, but I found that he, too, was gone.

With a light heart I turned down the side road through the deepening valley to which Johann had objected. There was not the slightest reason, that I could see, for his objection; and I daresay I tramped for a couple of hours without thinking of time or distance, and certainly without seeing a person or a house. So far as the place was concerned, it was desolation itself. But I did not notice this particularly till, on turning a bend in the road, I came upon a scattered fringe of wood; then I recognized that I had been impressed unconsciously by the desolation of the region through which I had passed.

I sat down to rest myself, and began to look around. It struck me that it was considerably colder than it had been at the commencement of my walk—a sort of sighing sound seemed to be around me with, now and then, high overhead, a sort of muffled roar. Looking upwards I noticed that great thick clouds were drifting rapidly across the sky from North to South at a great height. There were signs of coming storm in some lofty stratum of the air. I was a little chilly, and, thinking that it was the sitting still after the exercise of walking, I resumed my journey.

The ground I passed over was now much more pictur-esque. There were no striking objects that the eye might single out; but in all there was a charm of beauty. I took little heed of time and it was only when the deepening twilight forced itself upon me that I began to think of how I should find my way home. The brightness of the day had gone. The air was cold, and the drifting of clouds high overhead was more marked. They were accompanied by a sort of far-away rushing sound, through which seemed to come at intervals that mysterious cry which the driver had said came from a wolf. For a while I hesitated. I had said I would see the deserted village, so on I went, and presently came on a wide stretch of open coun-try, shut in by hills all around. Their sides were covered with trees which spread down to the plain, dotting, in clumps, the gentler slopes and hollows which showed here and there. I fol-lowed with my eye the winding of the road, and saw that it curved close to one of the densest of these clumps and was lost behind it.

As I looked there came a cold shiver in the air, and the snow began to fall. I thought of the miles and miles of bleak country I had passed, and then hurried on to seek the shelter of the wood in front. Darker and darker grew the sky, and faster and heavier fell the snow, till the earth before and around me was a glistening white carpet the farther edge of which was lost in misty vagueness. The road was here but crude, and when on the level its boundaries were not so marked, as when it passed through the cuttings; and in a little while I found that I must have strayed from it, for I missed underfoot the hard surface, and my feet sank deeper in the grass and moss. Then the wind grew stronger and blew with ever increasing force, till I was fain to run before it. The air became icy-cold, and in spite of my exercise I began to suffer. The snow was now falling so thickly and whirling around me in such rapid eddies that I could hardly keep my eyes open. Every now and then the heavens were torn asunder by vivid lightning, and in the flashes I could see ahead of me a great mass of trees, chiefly yew and cypress, all heavily coated with snow.

I was soon amongst the shelter of the trees, and there, in comparative silence, I could hear the rush of the wind high overhead. Presently the blackness of the storm had become merged in the darkness of the night. By-and-by the storm seemed to be passing away: it now only came in fierce puffs or blasts. At such moments the weird sound of the wolf appeared to be echoed by many similar sounds around me.

Now and again, through the black mass of drifting cloud, came a straggling ray of moonlight which lit up the expanse, and showed me that I was at the edge of a dense mass of cypress and yew trees. As the snow had ceased to fall, I walked out from the shelter and began to investigate more closely. It appeared to me that, amongst so many old foundations as I had passed, there might be still standing a house in which, though in ruins, I could find some sort of shelter for a while. As I skirted the edge of the copse, I found that a low wall encircled it, and following this I presently found an opening. Here the cypresses formed an alley leading up to a square mass of some kind of building. Just as I caught sight of this, however, the drifting clouds obscured the moon, and I passed up the path in darkness. The wind must have grown colder, for I felt myself shiver as I walked; but there was hope of shelter, and I groped my way blindly on.

I stopped, for there was a sudden stillness. The storm had passed; and, perhaps in sympathy with nature's silence, my heart seemed to cease to beat. But this was only momentarily; for suddenly the moonlight broke through the clouds showing me that I was in a graveyard, and that the square object before me was a great massive tomb of marble, as white as the snow that lay on and all around it. With the moonlight there came a fierce sigh of the storm which appeared to resume its course with a long, low howl, as of many dogs or wolves. I was awed and shocked, and felt the cold perceptibly grow upon me till it seemed to grip me by the heart. Then while the flood of moonlight still fell on the marble tomb, the storm gave further evidence of renewing, as though it was returning on its track. Impelled by some sort of fascination, I approached the sepulchre to see what it was, and why such a thing stood alone in such a place. I walked around it, and read, over the Doric door, in German:

COUNTESS DOLINGEN OF GRATZ
IN STYRIA
SOUGHT AND FOUND DEATH.
1801.

On the top of the tomb, seemingly driven through the solid marble—for the structure was composed of a few vast blocks of stone—was a great iron spike or stake. On going to the back I saw, graven in great Russian letters:

"The dead travel fast."

There was something so weird and uncanny about the whole thing that it gave me a turn and made me feel quite faint. I began to wish, for the first time, that I had taken Johann's advice. Here a thought struck me, which came under almost mysterious circumstances and with a terrible shock. This was Walpurgis Night!

Walpurgis Night, when, according to the belief of millions of people, the devil was abroad—when the graves were opened and the dead came forth and walked. When all evil things of earth and air and water held revel. This very place the driver had specially shunned. This was the depopulated village of centuries ago. This was where the suicide lay; and this was the place where I was alone—unmanned, shivering with cold in a shroud of snow with a wild storm gathering again upon me! It took all my philosophy, all the religion I had been taught, all my courage, not to collapse in a paroxysm of fright.

And now a perfect tornado burst upon me. The ground shook as though thousands of horses thundered across it; and this time the storm bore on its icy wings, not snow, but great hailstones which drove with such violence that they might have come from the thongs of Balearic slingers—hailstones that beat down leaf and branch and made the shelter of the cypresses of no more avail than though their stems were standing-corn. At the first I had rushed to the nearest tree; but I was soon fain to leave it and seek the only spot that seemed to afford refuge, the deep Doric doorway of the marble tomb. There, crouching against the massive bronze-door, I gained a certain amount of protection from the beating of the hailstones, for now they only drove against me as they ricochetted from the ground and the side of the marble.

As I leaned against the door, it moved slightly and opened inwards. The shelter of even a tomb was welcome in that pitiless tempest, and I was about to enter it when there came a flash of forked-lightning that lit up the whole expanse of the heavens. In the instant, as I am a living man, I saw, as my eyes were turned into the darkness of the tomb, a beautiful woman, with rounded cheeks and red lips, seemingly sleeping on a bier. As the thunder broke overhead, I was grasped as by the hand of a giant and hurled out into the storm. The whole thing was so sudden that, before I could realize the shock, moral as well as physical, I found the hailstones beating me down. At the same time I had a strange, dominating feeling that I was not alone. I looked towards the tomb. Just then there came another blinding flash, which seemed to strike the iron stake that surmounted the tomb and to pour through to the earth, blasting and crumbling the marble, as in a burst of flame. The dead woman rose for a moment of agony, while she was lapped in the flame, and her bitter scream of pain was drowned in the thundercrash. The last thing I heard was this mingling of dreadful sound, as again I was seized in the giant-grasp and dragged away, while the hailstones beat on me, and the air around seemed reverberant with the howling of wolves. The last sight that I remembered was a vague, white, moving mass, as if all the graves around me had sent out the phantoms of their sheeted dead, and that they were closing in on me through the white cloudiness of the driving hail.

      *   *   *   *   *

Gradually there came a sort of vague beginning of consciousness; then a sense of weariness that was dreadful. For a time I remembered nothing; but slowly my senses returned. My feet seemed positively racked with pain, yet I could not move them. They seemed to be numbed. There was an icy feeling at the back of my neck and all down my spine, and my ears, like my feet, were dead, yet in torment; but there was in my breast a sense of warmth which was, by comparison, delicious. It was as a nightmare—a physical nightmare, if one may use such an expression; for some heavy weight on my chest made it difficult for me to breathe.

This period of semi-lethargy seemed to remain a long time, and as it faded away I must have slept or swooned. Then came a sort of loathing, like the first stage of sea-sickness, and a wild desire to be free of something—I knew not what. A vast stillness enveloped me, as though all the world were asleep or dead—only broken by the low panting as of some animal close to me. I felt a warm rasping at my throat, then came a consciousness of the awful truth, which chilled me to the heart and sent the blood surging up through my brain. Some great animal was lying on me and now licking my throat. I feared to stir, for some instinct of prudence bade me lie still; but the brute seemed to realize that there was now some change in me, for it raised its head. Through my eyelashes I saw above me the two great flaming eyes of a gigantic wolf. Its sharp white teeth gleamed in the gaping red mouth, and I could feel its hot breath fierce and acrid upon me.

For another spell of time I remembered no more. Then I became conscious of a low growl, followed by a yelp, renewed again and again. Then, seemingly very far away, I heard a "Holloa! holloa!" as of many voices calling in unison. Cautiously I raised my head and looked in the direction whence the sound came; but the cemetery blocked my view. The wolf still continued to yelp in a strange way, and a red glare began to move round the grove of cypresses, as though following the sound. As the voices drew closer, the wolf yelped faster and louder. I feared to make either sound or motion. Nearer came the red glow, over the white pall which stretched into the darkness around me. Then all at once from beyond the trees there came at a trot a troop of horsemen bearing torches. The wolf rose from my breast and made for the cemetery. I saw one of the horsemen (soldiers by their caps and their long military cloaks) raise his carbine and take aim. A companion knocked up his arm, and I heard the ball whiz over my head. He had evidently taken my body for that of the wolf. Another sighted the animal as it slunk away, and a shot followed. Then, at a gallop, the troop rode forward—some towards me, others following the wolf as it disappeared amongst the snow-clad cypresses.

As they drew nearer I tried to move, but was powerless, although I could see and hear all that went on around me. Two or three of the soldiers jumped from their horses and knelt beside me. One of them raised my head, and placed his hand over my heart.

"Good news, comrades!" he cried. "His heart still beats!"

Then some brandy was poured down my throat; it put vigour into me, and I was able to open my eyes fully and look around. Lights and shadows were moving among the trees, and I heard men call to one another. They drew together, uttering frightened exclamations; and the lights flashed as the others came pouring out of the cemetery pell-mell, like men possessed. When the farther ones came close to us, those who were around me asked them eagerly:

"Well, have you found him?"

The reply rang out hurriedly:

"No! no! Come away quick—quick! This is no place to stay, and on this of all nights!"

"What was it?" was the question, asked in all manner of keys. The answer came variously and all indefinitely as though the men were moved by some common impulse to speak, yet were restrained by some common fear from giving their thoughts.

"It—it—indeed!" gibbered one, whose wits had plainly given out for the moment.

"A wolf—and yet not a wolf!" another put in shudderingly.

"No use trying for him without the sacred bullet," a third remarked in a more ordinary manner.

"Serve us right for coming out on this night! Truly we have earned our thousand marks!" were the ejaculations of a fourth.

"There was blood on the broken marble," another said after a pause—"the lightning never brought that there. And for him—is he safe? Look at his throat! See, comrades, the wolf has been lying on him and keeping his blood warm."

The officer looked at my throat and replied:

"He is all right; the skin is not pierced. What does it all mean? We should never have found him but for the yelping of the wolf."

"What became of it?" asked the man who was holding up my head, and who seemed the least panic-stricken of the party, for his hands were steady and without tremor. On his sleeve was the chevron of a petty officer.

"It went to its home," answered the man, whose long face was pallid, and who actually shook with terror as he glanced around him fearfully. "There are graves enough there in which it may lie. Come, comrades—come quickly! Let us leave this cursed spot."

The officer raised me to a sitting posture, as he uttered a word of command; then several men placed me upon a horse. He sprang to the saddle behind me, took me in his arms, gave the word to advance; and, turning our faces away from the cypresses, we rode away in swift military order.

As yet my tongue refused its office, and I was perforce silent. I must have fallen asleep; for the next thing I remembered was finding myself standing up, supported by a soldier on each side of me. It was almost broad daylight, and to the north a red streak of sunlight was reflected like a path of blood, over the waste of snow. The officer was telling the men to say nothing of what they had seen, except that they found an English stranger, guarded by a large dog.

"Dog! that was no dog," cut in the man who had exhibited such fear. "I think I know a wolf when I see one."

The young officer answered calmly, "I said a dog."

"Dog!" reiterated the other ironically. It was evident that his courage was rising with the sun; and, pointing to me, he said, "Look at his throat. Is that the work of a dog, master?"

Instinctively I raised my hand to my throat, and as I touched it I cried out in pain. The men crowded round to look, some stooping down from their saddles; and again there came the calm voice of the young officer:

"A dog, as I said. If aught else were said we should only be laughed at."

I was then mounted behind a trooper, and we rode on into the suburbs of Munich. Here we came across a stray carriage, into which I was lifted, and it was driven off to the Quatre Saisons—the young officer accompanying me, whilst a trooper followed with his horse, and the others rode off to their barracks.

When we arrived, Herr Delbrück rushed so quickly down the steps to meet me, that it was apparent he had been watching within. Taking me by both hands he solicitously led me in. The officer saluted me and was turning to withdraw, when I recognized his purpose, and insisted that he should come to my rooms. Over a glass of wine I warmly thanked him and his brave comrades for saving me. He replied simply that he was more than glad, and that Herr Delbrück had at the first taken steps to make all the searching party pleased; at which ambiguous utterance the maître d'hôtel smiled, while the officer pleaded duty and withdrew.

"But Herr Delbrück," I enquired, "how and why was it that the soldiers searched for me?"

He shrugged his shoulders, as if in depreciation of his own deed, as he replied:

"I was so fortunate as to obtain leave from the commander of the regiment in which I served, to ask for volunteers."

"But how did you know I was lost?" I asked.

"The driver came hither with the remains of his carriage, which had been upset when the horses ran away."

"But surely you would not send a search party of soldiers merely on this account?"

"Oh, no!" he answered, "but even before the coachman arrived, I had this telegram from the Boyar whose guest you are," and he took from his pocket a telegram which he handed to me, and I read:

Dracula's Guest

Bistritz.

Be careful of my guest—his safety is most precious to me. Should aught happen to him, or if he be missed, spare nothing to find him and ensure his safety. He is English and therefore adventurous. There are often dangers from snow and wolves and night. Lose not a moment if you suspect harm to him. I answer your zeal with my fortune.

DRACULA.

As I held the telegram in my hand, the room seemed to whirl around me; and if the attentive maître d'hôtel had not caught me, I think I should have fallen. There was something so strange in all this, something so weird and impossible to imagine, that there grew on me a sense of my being in some way the sport of opposite forces—the mere vague idea of which seemed in a way to paralyse me. I was certainly under some form of mysterious protection. From a distant country had come, in the very nick of time, a message that took me out of the danger of the snow-sleep and the jaws of the wolf.

In the year 1915

17 Jan.	Russia defeats Ottoman forces at the Battle of Sarikamish (Caucasus campaign in Russia).
18 Jan.	The Twenty-One Demands of Japan are presented to the Republic of China.
24 Jan.	The Battle of Dogger Bank: the British Grand Fleet defeats the German High Seas Fleet.
22 April	Beginning of the Second Battle of Ypres. First mass use of poison gas by Germany on the Western Front.
25 April	Allied forces begin their land invasion of the Gallipoli peninsula in the Ottoman Empire.
26 April	Italy secretly agrees to leave the Triple Alliance and join with the Entente Powers.
3 May	Canadian soldier John McCrae writes the poem "In Flanders Fields."
7 May	The British ocean liner RMS *Lusitania* is sunk by Imperial German Navy U-boat *U-20*, killing approximately 1,195 civilians en route from New York City to Liverpool.
23 May	Italy declares war on the Austro-Hungarian Empire.
27 May	Promulgation of the Tehcir Law in the Ottoman Empire, authorising the deportation of the Armenian population.
14 Oct.	Bulgaria enters World War I and invades Serbia.
18 Oct.	Germany establishes the Government General of Warsaw in north-west Poland following the retreat of Russian forces.
12 Dec.	Yuan Shikai declares himself Emperor of China.
15 Dec.	Beginning of the evacuation of ANZAC forces from the Gallipoli peninsula.

— 1915 —

The White Hare

Bernard Capes

Raven Speaks

You know the Mendips or you don't know them—their beauty, their savagery, their wide-flung loneliness sweeping miles down into the haunted valley called the moors, where, in the moonlit nights, strange craft come floating from Glastonbury on mystic waters long since sunk and lost. There may be trippers in this place and that to vulgarise the brooding hours, and if you see with their eyes you see nothing; but they are local, after all—mere profaners of places already profaned to show. One may leave them behind, to resettle like flies disturbed from carrion, and, entering into the fastnesses of the hills, forget them in a moment.

The place belongs to legend and the past; it murmurs with inarticulate voices, drums and rustles under visionary footfalls. Once, long ago there stood a little ruined church, difficult to strangers to find, among the high, far thickets, and there the dead lay tumbled and neglected, because the building had been desecrated of old, and never since reconsecrated; so that it was avoided by the people, and the fence surrounding the grave-yard rotted piecemeal and grew choked with fungus and brier.

There was an evening when young Modred, abroad with his gun, found himself benighted, a little cold, but curious, near that thicket—and suddenly a white hare slipped from the palings, and ran before him like a jumping snowball. He fired on the instant, and could have sworn his unerring eye had not failed him; but the hare ran on and melted, verily like snow, into the glooms. He was startled, awed, but not to be browbeaten by puss or devil. Another evening he sought the place, sighted his quarry, and again failed inexplicably to bring her down. Then he remembered—white hare, white witch—silver alone could prevail against the cursed thing. On the third evening therefore he loaded with a silver button from his coat, a keepsake from his maiden love, and, biding his time, let fly at the loping succuba. There was a scream like a woman's— and the hare sped on and vanished. But she was hit at last.

The next day Modred learned that his love was dead. She had taken down her father's gun, not knowing it was loaded, to clean, and by some means the charge had been exploded into her breast.

Hideous the tragedy; hideous the moral to be drawn from it. From that time the man went like a mad thing, his heart broken, his soul an alien from earth and heaven. That it should have been she, and her gift to him her death! But most he raved against the cynic God, who might have ordered things differently, but would have them thus and thus to make sport for himself.

And then the dead girl's mother came to die; but she could not die; and she screamed and stormed on life to let her go; but life held her still fast in her agony. Then one day she sent for Modred.

"Cut the cursed thing from my shoulder," she said, "and let me pass."

"What thing?" he asked stupefied.

There was a scream like a woman's—and the hare sped on and vanished. But she was hit at last.

"Your silver button," she said, "that mauled, but could not end me. It has lain there ever since, keeping me from the churchyard and my friends the outlawed dead. I killed the innocent girl myself to mislead you, and I bore the pain of this, until now I cannot bear it. Cut it out."

Her shoulder was bare, and the button stood under the skin of it like a little blue plum. Modred, with a howl of fury, took it in his fingers and tore it away.

At that the woman screeched and fell, and out of the window leapt a white hare and vanished up the hill.

In the year 1916

21 Feb.	Beginning of the Battle of Verdun in France. The French repulse a major German offensive.
9 March	Mexican general Francisco "Pancho" Villa leads an attack on Columbus, New Mexico.
22 March	J.R.R. Tolkien and Edith Bratt marry at St Mary Immaculate Roman Catholic Church, Warwick, England.
22 March	Yuan Shikai abdicates and the Republic of China is restored.
24–29 April	Easter Rising: Irish republicans launch an insurrection against British rule.
31 May	Beginning of the Battle of Jutland between Britain and Germany in the North Sea.
4 June	Beginning of the Brusilov Offensive by Russia on the Eastern Front.
5 June	The HMS *Hampshire* hits a mine off the Orkney Islands; 737 people are killed, including Field Marshal Lord Kitchener, British Secretary of State for War.
10 June	The Arab Revolt against the Ottoman Empire officially begins at Mecca.
1 July	Beginning of the Battle of the Somme, a joint British-French offensive against German forces.
27 Aug.	Romania declares war on the Central Powers.
5 Nov.	The Kingdom of Poland is proclaimed by the German Empire and Austro-Hungarian Empire.
7 Nov.	Woodrow Wilson narrowly wins the USA Presidential Election, defeating Republican candidate Charles Evans Hughes.
30 Dec.	Russian mystic Grigori Yefimovich Rasputin is murdered in Petrograd (Saint Petersburg).

— 1916 —

The Haunted Pampero

William Hope Hodgson

I.

"Hurrah!" cried young Tom Pemberton as he threw open the door and came forward into the room where his newlywed wife was busily employed about some sewing, "they've given me a ship. What ho!" and he threw his peaked uniform cap down on the table with a bang.

"A ship, Tom?" said his wife, letting her sewing rest idly on her lap.

"The *Pampero*!" said Tom proudly.

"What! The 'Haunted *Pampero*'?" cried his wife in a voice expressive of more dismay than elation.

"That's what a lot of fools call her," admitted Tom, unwilling to hear a word against his new kingdom. "It's all a lot of rot! She's no more haunted than I am!"

"And you've accepted?" asked Mrs. Tom, anxiously, rising to her feet with a sudden movement which sent the contents of her lap to the floor.

"You bet I have!" replied Tom. "It's not a chance to be thrown away, to be Master of a vessel before I've jolly well reached twenty-five."

He went toward her, holding out his arms happily; but he stopped suddenly as he caught sight of the dismayed look upon her face.

"What's up, little girl?" he asked. "You don't look a bit pleased." His voice denoted that her lack of pleasure in his news hurt him.

"I'm not, Tom. Not a bit. She's a dreadful ship! All sorts of horrible things happen to her—"

"Rot!" interrupted Tom decisively. "What do you know about her anyway? She's one of the finest vessels in the company."

"Everybody knows," she said, with a note of tears in her voice. "Oh, Tom, can't you get out of it?"

"Don't want to!" crossly.

"Why didn't you come and ask me before deciding?"

"Wasn't any time!" gruffly. "It was 'Yes' or 'No'."

"Oh, why didn't you say 'No'?"

"Because I'm not a fool!" growing savage.

"I shall never be happy again," she said, sitting down abruptly and beginning to cry.

Tears had their due effect, and the next instant Tom was kneeling beside her, libelling himself heartily. Presently, after sundry passages, her nose—a little pink—came out from the depths of *his* handkerchief.

"I shall come with you!" The words were uttered with sufficient determination to warn him that there was real danger of her threat being put into execution, and Tom, who was not entirely free from the popular superstition regarding the *Pampero*, began to feel uneasy as she combated every objection which he put forward. It was all very well going to sea in her himself, but to take his little girl, well—that was another thing. And so, like a sensible loving fellow, he fought every inch of the ground with her; the natural result being that at the end of an hour he retired—shall we say "retreated"—to smoke a pipe in his den and meditate on the perversity of womankind in general and his own wife in particular.

And she—well, she went to her bedroom, and turned out all her pretty summer dresses, and for a time was quite happy. No doubt she was thinking of the tropics. Later, under Tom's somewhat disparaging guidance, she made selection among her more substantial frocks. And, in short, three weeks later saw her at sea in the haunted *Pampero*, along with her husband.

II.

The first ten days, aided by a fresh fair wind, took them well clear of the Channel, and Mrs. Tom Pemberton was beginning to find her sea legs. Then, on the thirteenth day out they ran into dirty weather. Hitherto, the *Pampero* had been lucky (for her), nothing special having occurred save that one of the men was laid up through the starboard fore crane line having given way under him, letting him down on deck with a run. Yet, because the man was alive and no limbs broken, there was a general feeling that the old packet was on her good behaviour.

Then, as I have said, they ran into bad weather and were hove to for three weary days under bare poles. On the morning of the fourth, the wind moderated sufficiently to allow of their setting the main top-sail, storm foresail, and staysail, and running her off before the wind. During that day the weather grew steadily finer, the wind dropping and the sea going down; so that by evening they were bowling along before a comfortable six-knot breeze. Then, just before sunset, they had evidence once again that the *Pampero* was on her good behaviour, and that there were other ships less lucky than she; for out of the red glare of sunset to starboard[1] there floated to them the water-logged shell of a ship's lifeboat.

---

1   The right side of a ship when facing the bow (front), cf. port (left).

In passing, one of the men caught a glimpse of something crumpled up on a thwart,[2] and sung out to the Mate who was in charge. He, having obtained permission from the Skipper,[3] put the ship in irons and lowered a boat. Reaching the wrecked craft, it was discovered that the something on the thwart was the still living form of a seaman, exhausted and scarcely in his right mind. Evidently they had been only just in time; for hardly had they removed him to their own boat before the other, with a slow, oily roll, disappeared from sight.

They returned with him to the ship, where he was made comfortable in a spare bunk; and on the next day, being sufficiently recovered, told how that he had been one of the A.B.'s[4] in the *Cyclops*, and how that she had broached to while running before the gale two nights previously, and gone down with all hands. He had found himself floating beside her battered lifeboat, which had evidently been torn from its place on the skids as the ship capsized; he had managed to get hold of the lifelines and climb into her, and since then, how he had managed to exist, he could not say.

Two days later, the man who had fallen through the breaking of the crane line expired, at which some of the crew were uneasy, declaring that the old packet was going back on them.

"It's as I said," remarked one of the Ordinaries, "she's 'er bloomin', 'aunted tin kettle, an' if it weren't better being 'aunted 'n 'ungry, I'd bloomin' well stay ashore!" Therein he may be said to have voiced the general sentiments of the rest.

With this man dying, Captain Tom Pemberton offered to sign on Tarpin—the man they had picked up—in his place. Tarpin thankfully accepted, and took the dead man's place in

---

2   A transverse wooden seat in a rowing boat.

3   The captain.

4   Able seaman: denoting an ordinary seaman with experience.

the fo'cas'le,[5] for, though undeniably an old man, he was, as he had already shown on a couple of occasions, a smart sailor.

He was specially adept at rope splicing, and had a peculiarly shaped marlinspike, from which he was never separated. It served him as a weapon too, and occasionally some of the crew thought he drew it too freely.

And now it appeared that the ship's bad genius was determined to prove that it was by no means so black as it had been painted; for matters went on quietly and evenly for two complete weeks, during which the ship wandered across the line into the Southern Tropics, and there slid into one of those hateful calms which lurk there remorselessly awaiting their prey.

For two days Captain Tom Pemberton whistled vainly for wind; on the third he swore (under his breath when his wife was about, otherwise when she was below). On the evening of the fourth day he ceased to say naughty words about the lack of wind, for something happened, something altogether inexplicable and frightening; so much so that he was careful to tell his wife nothing concerning the matter, she being below at the time.

The sun had set some minutes and the evening was dwindling rapidly into night, when from for'ard there came a tremendous uproar of pigs squealing and shrieking.

Captain Tom and the Second Mate, who were pacing the poop together, stopped in their promenade and listened.

"Damnation!" exclaimed the Captain. "Who's messing with the pigs?"

The Second Mate was proceeding to roar out to one of the 'prentices to jump forward and see what was up when a man came running aft to say that there was something in the pigsty getting at the pigs, and would he come forward. On hearing

---

5   Forecastle: the area under the forward deck of a ship that serves as living quarters for sailors.

this, the Captain and the Second Mate went forward at a run. As they passed along the deck and came nearer to the sound of action, they distinctly heard the sound of savage snarling mingled with the squealing of the pigs.

"What the devil's that!" gasped the Second, as he tried to keep pace with the Skipper. Then they were by the pigsty, and, in the gathering gloom, found the crew grouped in a semi-circle foreside the sty.

"What's up?" roared Captain Tom Pemberton. "What's up here?" He made a way through the men, and stooped and peered through the iron bars of the sty, but it was too dark to make out anything with certainty. Then, before he could take away his face, there came a deeper, fiercer growl, and something snapped between the bars. The Captain gave out a cry and jumped back among the men, holding his nose.

"Hurt, Sir?" asked the Second Mate anxiously.

"N-no," said the Captain in a scared, doubtful voice. He fingered his nose for a further moment or two. "I don't think so."

The Second Mate turned and caught the nearest man by the shoulder.

"Bring out one of your lamps, smart now!" Yet even as he spoke, one of the Ordinaries came running out with one ready lighted. The Second snatched it from him and held it toward the pigsty. In the same instant something wet and shiny struck it from his hand. The Second Mate gave a shout, and then there was an instant's quietness in which all caught a sound of something slithering curiously along the decks to leeward.[6] Several of the men made a run to the fo'cas'le, but the Second was on his knees groping for the lantern. He found it and struck a light. The pigs had stopped squealing, but were still grunting in an agitated manner. He held the lantern near the bars and looked.

---

6   The side of a ship sheltered from the wind, cf. 'windward'.

Two of the pigs were huddled up in the starboard corner of the sty, and they were bleeding in several places. The third, a big fellow, was stretched upon his back; he had been bitten terribly about the throat and was quite dead.

The Captain put his hand on the Second's shoulder and stooped forward to get a better view.

"My God, Mister Kasson, what's been here," he muttered with an air of consternation.

The men had drawn up close behind and around and were now looking on, almost too astonished to venture opinions. Then a man's voice broke the momentary silence:

"Looks as if they 'ad been 'avin' a 'op with a cussed great shark!"

The Second Mate moved the light along before the bars. "The door's shut and the toggel's on, Sir," he said in a low voice.

The Skipper grasped his meaning but said nothing.

"S'posin' it 'ad been one o' us," muttered a man behind him.

From the surrounding "crowd" there came a murmur of comprehension and some uneasy glancing from side to side and behind.

The Skipper faced round upon them.

He opened his mouth to speak; then shut it as though a sudden idea had come to him.

"That light, quickly, Mister Kasson!" he exclaimed, holding out his hand.

The Second passed him the lamp, and he held it above his head. He was counting the men. They were all there, watch below and watch on deck; even the man on the lookout had come running down. There was absent only the man at the wheel.

He turned to the Second Mate.

"Take a couple of the men aft with you, Mister Kasson, and pass out some lamps. We must make a search!"

In a couple of minutes they returned with a dozen lighted lamps, which were quickly distributed among the men; then a thorough search of the decks was commenced. Every corner was peered into; but nothing found, and so, at last, they had to give it up, unsuccessful.

"That'll do, men," said Captain Tom. "Hang one of those lamps up foreside the pigsty and shove the others back in the locker." Then he and the Second Mate went aft.

At the bottom of the poop[7] steps the Skipper stopped abruptly and said, "Hush!" For a half a minute they listened, but without being able to say that they had heard anything definite. Then Captain Tom Pemberton turned and continued his way up on to the poop.

"What was it, Sir?" asked the Second, as he joined him at the top of the ladder.

"I'm hanged if I know!" replied Captain Tom. "I feel all adrift. I never heard there was anything—anything like this!"

"And we've no dogs aboard!"

"Dogs! More like tigers. Did you hear what one of the shellbacks[8] said?"

"A shark, you mean, Sir?" said the Second Mate, with some remonstrance in his tone.

"Have you ever seen a shark-bite, Mister Kasson?"

"No, Sir," replied the Second Mate.

"Those are shark-bites, Mister Kasson! God help us! Those are shark-bites!"

---

7   Poop deck, deck that forms the roof of a cabin built in the rear ("aft") of a ship.

8   Veteran sailor.

Evidently they had been only just in time; for hardly had they removed him to their own boat before the other, with a slow, oily roll, disappeared from sight.

III.

After this inexplicable affair a week of stagnant calm passed without anything unusual happening, and Captain Tom Pemberton was gradually losing the sense of haunting fear which had been so acute during the nights following the death of the porker.

It was early night, and Mrs. Tom Pemberton was sitting in a deck chair on the weather side of the saloon skylight near the for'ard end. The Captain and the First Mate were walking up and down, passing and repassing her. Presently the Captain stopped abruptly in his walk, leaving the Mate to continue along the deck. Then, crossing quietly to where his wife was sitting, he bent over her.

"What is it, dear?" he asked. "I've seen you once or twice looking to leeward as though you heard something. What is it?"

His wife sat forward and caught his arm.

"Listen!" she said in a sharp undertone. "There it is again! I've been thinking it must be my fancy; but it isn't. Can't you hear it?"

Captain Tom was listening, and just as his wife spoke, his strained sense caught a low, snarling growl from among the shadows to leeward. Though he gave a start he said nothing; but his wife saw his hand steal to his side pocket.

"You heard it?" she said eagerly. Then, without waiting for an answer: "Do you know, Tom, I've heard the sound three times already. It's just like an animal growling somewhere over there," and she pointed among the shadows. She was so positive about having heard it that her husband gave up all idea of trying to make her believe that her imagination had been playing tricks with her. Instead, he caught her hand and raised her to her feet.

"Come below, Annie," he said, and led her to the companion-way.[9] There he left her for a moment, and ran across to where the First Mate was on the look out; then back to her and led her down the stairs. In the saloon she turned and faced him.

"What was it, Tom? You're afraid of something, and you're keeping it from me. It's something to do with this horrible vessel!"

The Captain stared at her with a puzzled look. He did not know how much or how little to tell her. Then, before he could speak, she had stepped to his side and thrust her hand into the side pocket of his coat on the right.

"You've got a pistol!" she cried, pulling the weapon out with a jerk. "That shows it's something you're frightened of! It's something dangerous, and you won't tell me. I shall come up on deck with you again!" She was almost tearful and very much in earnest; so much so that the Captain turned-to and told her everything, which was, after all, the wisest thing he could have done under the circumstances.

"Now," he said, when he had made an end, "you must promise never to come up on deck at night without me—now promise!"

"I will, dear, if you will promise to be careful and—and not run any risks. Oh, I wish you hadn't taken this horrid ship!" And she commenced to cry.

Later, she consented to be quieted, and the Captain left her after having exacted a promise from her that she would "turn in" right away and get some sleep.

The first part she fulfilled without delay; but the latter was more difficult, and at least an hour went by tediously before at last, growing drowsy, she fell into an uneasy sleep. From this she was awakened some little time later with a start. She had seemed to hear some noise. Her bunk was up against the

---

9   A hatchway with a stair or ladder leading below decks.

side of the ship, and a glass port opened right above it, and it was from this port that the noise proceeded. It was a queer slurring sort of noise, as though something were rubbing up against it, and she grew frightened as she listened; for though she had pushed the port to on getting into her bunk, she was by no means certain that she had slipped the screw-catch on properly. She was, however, a plucky little woman, and wasted no time; but made one jump to the floor, and ran to the lamp. Turning it up with a sudden, nervous movement, she glanced towards the port. Behind the thick circle of glass she made out something that seemed to be pressed up against it. A queer, curved indentation ran right across it. Abruptly, as she stared, it gaped, and teeth flashed into sight. The whole thing started to move up and down across the glass, and she heard again that queer slurring noise which had frightened her into wakefulness. The thought leaped across her mind, as though it were a revelation, that it was something living, and it was grubbing at the glass, trying to get in. She put a hand down on to the table to steady herself, and tried to think.

Behind her the cabin door opened softly, and someone came into the room. She heard her husband's voice say: "Why, Annie—" in a tone of astonishment, and then stop dead. The next instant a sharp report filled the little cabin with sound and the glass of the port was starred all across, and there was no more anything of which to be afraid, for Captain Tom's arms were round her.

From the door there came a noise of loud knocking and the voice of the First Mate:

"Anything wrong, Sir?"

"It's all right, Mister Stennings. I'll be with you in half a minute." He heard the Mate's footsteps retreat, and go up the companion ladder. Then he listened quietly as his wife told him her story. When she had made an end, they sat and talked awhile gravely, with an infinite sense of being upon the borders of the Unknown. Suddenly a noise out upon the deck interrupted their talk, a man crying aloud with terror, and then a pistol shot and the Mate's voice shouting. Captain Pemberton leaped to his feet simultaneously with his wife.

"Stay here, Annie!" he commanded, and pushed her down onto the seat. He turned to the door; then an idea coming to him, he ran back and thrust his revolver into her hands. "I'll be with you in a minute," he said assuringly; then, seizing a heavy cutlass from the rack on the bulkhead, he opened the door and made a run for the deck.

His wife, on her part, at once hurried to make sure that the port catch was properly on. She saw that it was, and made haste to screw it up tightly. As she did so, she noticed that the bullet had passed clean through the glass on the left-hand side, low down. Then she returned to her seat with the revolver and sat listening and waiting.

On the main-deck the Captain found the Mate and a couple of men just below the break of the poop. The rest of the watch were gathered in a clump a little foreside of them, and between them and the Mate stood one of the 'prentices, holding a binnacle[10] lamp. The two men with the Mate were Coalson and Tarpin. Coalson appeared to be saying something. Tarpin was nursing his jaw and seemed to be in considerable pain.

"What is it, Mister Stennings?" sang out the Skipper quietly.

The First Mate glanced up.

"Will you come down, Sir," he said. "There's been some infernal devilment on!"

Even as he spoke the Captain was in the act of running down the poop ladder. Reaching the Mate and the two men, he put a few questions rapidly and learned that Coalson had been on his way aft to relieve the "wheel," when all at once something had leaped out at him from under the lee pin-rail.

---

10 A stand on the deck of a ship which holds navigational instruments.

Fortunately, he had turned just in time to avoid it, and then, shouting at the top of his voice, had run for his life. The Mate had heard him and, thinking he saw something behind, had fired. Almost directly afterward they had heard Tarpin calling out further for'ard, and then he too had come running aft; but just under the skids he had caught his foot in a ring-bolt, and come crashing to the deck, smashing his face badly against the sharp corner of the after-hatch. He, too, it would appear, had been chased; but by what, he could not say. Both the men were greatly agitated and could only tell their stories jerkily and with some incoherence.

With a certain feeling of the hopelessness of it all, Captain Pemberton gave orders to get lanterns and search the decks; but, as he anticipated, nothing unusual was found. Yet the bringing out of the lanterns suggested a wise precaution; for he told them to keep out a couple, and carry them about with them when they went to and fro along the decks.

IV.

Two nights later, Captain Pemberton was suddenly aroused from a sound sleep by his wife.

"Shish!" she whispered, putting her fingers on his lips. "Listen!"

He rose on his elbow, but otherwise kept quiet. The berth was full of shadows for the lamp was turned rather low. A minute of tense silence passed; then abruptly from the direction of the door, he heard a slow, gritty rubbing noise. At that he sat upright and sliding his hand beneath his pillow, brought out his revolver; then remained silent—waiting.

Suddenly he heard the latch of the door snick softly out of its catch, and an instant later a breath of air swept through the berth, stirring the draperies. By that he knew that the door had been opened, and he leaned forward, raised his weapon.

A moment of intense stillness followed; then, all at once, something dark slid between him and the little glimmer of flame in the lamp. Instantly he aimed and fired, once—twice. There came a hideous howling which seemed to be retreating toward the door, and he fired in the direction of the noise. He heard it pass into the saloon. Then came a quick slither of steps upon the companion stairway, and the noise died away into silence.

Immediately afterward, the Skipper heard the Mate bellowing for the watch to lay aft; then his heavy tread came tumbling down into the saloon, and the Captain, who had left his bunk to turn up his lamp, met him in the doorway. A minute was sufficient to put the Mate in possession of such facts as the Skipper himself had gleaned, and after that, they lit the saloon lamp and examined the floor and companion stairs. In several places they found traces of blood which showed that one, at least, of Captain Tom's shots had got home. They were also found to lead a little way along the lee side of the poop; but ceased altogether nearly opposite the end of the skylight.

As may be imagined, this affair had given the Captain a big shaking up, and he felt so little like attempting further sleep that he proceeded to dress; an action which his wife imitated, and the two of them passed the rest of the night on the poop; for, as Mrs. Pemberton said: "You felt safer up in the fresh air. You could at least feel that you were near help." A sentiment which, probably, Captain Tom *felt* more distinctly than he could have put into words. Yet he had another thought of which he was much more acutely aware, and which he did manage to formulate in some shape to the Mates during the course of the following day. As he put it:

"It's my wife that I'm afraid for! That thing (whatever it is) seems to be making a dead set for her!" His face was anxious and somewhat haggard under the tan. The two Mates nodded.

"I should keep a man in the saloon at night, Sir," suggested the Second Mate, after a moment's thought. "And let her keep with you as much as possible."

Captain Tom Pemberton nodded with a slight air of relief. The reasonableness of the precaution appealed to him. He would have a man in the saloon after dark, and he would see that the lamp was kept going; then, at least, his wife would be safe, for the only entrance to his cabin was through the saloon. As for the shattered port, it had been replaced the day after he had broken it, and now every dog watch[11] he saw to it himself that it was securely screwed up, and not only that, but the iron storm-cover as well; so that he had no fears in that direction.

That night at eight o'clock, as the roll was being called, the Second Mate turned and beckoned respectfully to the Captain, who immediately left his wife and stepped up to him.

"About that man, Sir?" said the Second. "I'm up here till twelve o'clock. Who would you care to have out of my watch?"

"Just as you like, Mister Kasson. Who can you best spare?"

"Well, Sir, if it comes to that, there's old Tarpin. He's not been much use on a rope since that tumble he got the other night. He hurt his arm as well, for he's not able to use it."

"Very well, Mister Kasson. Tell him to step up."

This the Second Mate did, and in a few moments old Tarpin stood before them. His face was bandaged up, and his right arm was slipped out of the sleeve of his coat.

"You seem to have been in the wars, Tarpin," said the Skipper, eyeing him up and down.

"Yes, Sir," replied the man, with a touch of grimness.

"I want you down in the saloon till twelve o'clock," the Captain went on. "If you—er—hear anything, call me, do you hear?"

---

11   The first "dog watch" (work shift on a ship) is from 16:00 until 18:00 and the second is from 18:00 until 20:00.

The man gave out a gruff "aye, aye, Sir," and went slowly aft.

"I don't expect he's best pleased, Sir," said the Second with a slight smile.

"How do you mean, Mister Kasson?"

"Well, Sir, ever since he and Coalson were chased, and he got the tumble, he's taken to waiting around the decks at night. He seems a plucky old devil, and it's my belief he's waiting to get square with whatever it was that made him run."

"Then he's just the man I want in the saloon," said the Skipper. "It may just happen that he gets his chance of coming close to quarters with this infernal hell-thing that's knocking about. And, by Jove, if he does, he and I'll be friends for evermore."

At nightfall Captain Tom Pemberton and his wife went below. They found old Tarpin sitting on one of the benches. At their entrance he rose to his feet and touched his cap awkwardly to them. The Captain stopped a moment and spoke to him:

"Mind, Tarpin, the least sound of anything about, and call me! And see you keep the lamp bright."

"Aye, aye, Sir," said the man quietly; and the Skipper left him and followed his wife into their cabin.

V.

The Captain had been asleep more than an hour when abruptly something roused him. He reached for his revolver and then sat upright; yet though he listened intently, no sound came to him save the gentle breathing of his wife. The lamp was low, but not so low that he could not make out the various details of the cabin. His glance roved swiftly round and showed him nothing unusual, until it came to the door; then, in a flash, he noted that no light from the saloon lamp came under the bottom. He jumped swiftly from his bunk with a sudden gust of anger. If Tarpin had gone to sleep and allowed the lamp to go out, well—! His hand was upon the key. He had taken the precaution to turn it before going to sleep. How providential this action had been he was soon to learn. In the very act of unlocking the door he paused; for all at once a low grumbling purr came to him from beyond the door. Ah! That was the sound that had come to him in his sleep and wakened him. For a moment he stood, a multitude of frightened fancies coming to him. Then, realizing that now was such a chance as he might not have again, he turned the key with a swift movement and flung the door wide open.

The first thing he noticed was that the saloon lamp had burned down and was flickering, sending uncomfortable splashes of light and darkness across the place. The next, that something lay at his feet across the threshold—something that started up with a snarl and turned upon him. He pushed the muzzle of his revolver against it and pulled the trigger twice. The Thing gave out a queer roar and flung itself from him half-way across the saloon floor; then it rose to a semi-upright position and darted howling through the doorway leading to the companion stairs. Behind him he heard his wife crying out in alarm; but he did not stay to answer her; instead, he followed the Thing voicing its pains so hideously. At the bottom of the stairs he glanced up and saw something outlined against the stars. It was only a glimpse, and he saw that it had two legs, like a man; yet he thought of a shark. It disappeared, and he leaped up the stairs. He stared to the leeward and saw something by the rail. As he fired, the Thing leaped and a cry and a splash came almost simultaneously. The Second Mate joined him breathlessly, as he raced to his side.

"What was it, Sir?" gasped the officer.

"Look!" shouted Captain Tom, pointing down into the dark sea.

He stared down into the glassy darkness. Something like a great fish showed below the surface. It was dimly outlined by the phosphorescence. It was swimming in an erratic circle leaving an indistinct trail of glowing bubbles behind it. Something caught the Second Mate's eyes as he stared, and he leaned farther out so as to get a better view. He saw the Thing again. The fish had two tails—or they might have been legs. The Thing was swimming downward. How rapidly, he could judge by the speed at which its apparent size diminished. He turned and caught the Captain by the wrist.

"Do you see its—its tails, Sir?" he muttered excitedly. Captain Tom Pemberton gave an unintelligible grunt, but kept his eyes fixed on the deep. The Second glanced back. Far below him he made out a little moving spot of phosphorescence. It grew fainter, and vanished in the immensity beneath them.

Someone touched the Captain on the arm. It was his wife.

"Oh, Tom, have you—have you—?" she began; but he said "Hush!" and turned to the Second Mate.

"Call all hands, Mister Kasson!" he ordered; then, taking his wife by the arm, he led her down with him into the saloon. Here they found the Steward in his shirt and trousers, trimming the lamp. His face was pale, and he started to question as soon as they entered; but the Captain quieted him with a gesture.

"Look in all the empty cabins!" the Skipper commanded, and while the Steward was doing this, the Skipper himself made a search of the saloon floor. In a few minutes the Steward came up to say that the cabins were as usual, whereupon the Captain led his wife on deck. Here the Second Mate met them.

"The hands are mustered, Sir," he said.

"Very good, Mister Kasson. Call the roll!"

The roll was gone over, each man answering to his name in turn. The Second Mate reached the last three on the list.

"Jones!"

"Sir!"

"Smith!"

"Yessir!"

"Tarpin!"

But from the waiting crowd below, in the light of the Second Mate's lantern, no answer came. He called the name again, and then Captain Tom Pemberton touched him on the arm. He turned and looked at the Captain, whose eyes were full of incredible realization.

"It's no good, Mister Kasson," the Captain said. "I had to make quite sure—"

He paused, and the Second Mate took a step towards him.

"But—where is he?" he asked, almost stupidly.

The Captain leaned forward, looking him in the eyes.

"You saw him go, Mister Kasson!" he said in a low voice.

The Second Mate stared back, but he did not see the Captain. Instead, he saw again in his mind's eye two things that looked like legs—human legs!

There was no more trouble that voyage; no more strange happenings; nothing unusual; but Captain Tom Pemberton had no peace of mind until he reached port and his wife was safely ashore again.

The story of the *Pampero*, her bad reputation, and this latest extraordinary happening got into the papers. Among the many articles which the tale evoked was one which held certain interesting suggestions.

The writer quoted from an old manuscript, entitled "Ghosts", the well-known legend of the sea-ghoul—which, as will be remembered, asserts that those who "*die by ye sea, live of ye sea, and do come upward upon lonely shores, and do eate, biting like ye shark or ye deyvel-fishe, and are drywdful in hunger for ye fleyshe of man, and, moreover, do strive in mid sea to board ye ships of ye deep water, that they shal saytisfy theire dryedful hunger.*"

The author of the article suggested seriously that the man Tarpin was some abnormal thing out of the profound deeps; that had destroyed those who had once been in the whale-boat, and afterward, with dreadful cunning, been taken aboard the *Pampero* as a castaway, afterward indulging its monstrous appetite. What form of life the creature possessed, the writer frankly could not indicate, but set out the uncomfortable suggestion that the case of the *Pampero* was not the first; nor would it be the last. He reminded the public of the many ships that vanish. He pointed out how a ship, thus dreadfully bereft of her crew, might founder and sink when the first heavy storm struck her.

He concluded his article by asserting his opinion that he did not believe the *Pampero* to be "haunted." It was, he held, simple chance that had associated a long tale of ill-luck with the vessel in question; and that the thing which had happened could have happened as easily to any other vessel which might have met and picked up the grim occupant of the derelict whale-boat.

Whatever may be the correctness of the writer's suggestions, they are at least interesting in endeavouring to sum up this extraordinary and incomprehensible happening. But Captain Pemberton felt surer of his own sanity when he remembered (when he thought of the matter at all) that men often go mad from exposure in open boats, and that the marlinspike which Tarpin always carried was sharpened much to the shape of a shark's tooth.

In the year 1917

5 Feb.	The Mexican Constitution is ratified.
8 March	The February Revolution (23 February in the Julian calendar) begins in Petrograd, Russia, and lasts for eight days.
11 March	Venustiano Carranza of the Liberal Constitutionalist Party is elected president of Mexico.
15 March	Tsar Nicholas II of Russia abdicates, marking the end of the Russian Empire.
26 March	First Battle of Gaza in Palestine: first attempt by the British to take Gaza from Ottoman forces.
6 April	The USA declares war on Germany.
17 April	London newspapers *The Times* and *The Daily Mail* print false claims of a "German Corpse Factory" for rendering of corpses into tallow.
7 June	The Battle of Messines: the British Army detonates nineteen mines under German lines.
July	The first Cottingley Fairy photographs are taken in England by Elsie Wright and Frances Griffiths. The hoax takes in Arthur Conan Doyle.
6 July	Arab troops led by British officer T.E. Lawrence capture Aqaba from the Ottoman Empire.
31 July	The Third Battle of Ypres (Battle of Passchendaele) begins in Belgium.
2 Nov.	Foreign Secretary Arthur Balfour proclaims British support for the establishment of a Jewish homeland in Palestine.
7 Nov.	The October Revolution: Bolsheviks seize power in Petrograd, Russia.
17 Nov.	The Battle of Jerusalem: the British Egyptian Expeditionary Force attacks Ottoman forces in the Judaean Hills and around Jerusalem.

— 1917 —

The Coming of the Terror

Arthur Machen

After two years we are turning once more to the morning's news with a sense of appetite and glad expectation. There were thrills at the beginning of the war, the thrill of horror and of a doom that seemed at once incredible and certain. This was when Namur fell, and the German host swelled like a flood over the French fields, and drew very near to the walls of Paris. Then we felt the thrill of exultation when the good news came that the awful tide had been turned back, that Paris and the world were safe, for a while, at all events.

Then for days we hoped for more news as good as this or better. Has Kluck been surrounded? Not today, but perhaps he will be surrounded tomorrow. But the days became weeks, the weeks drew out to months; the battle in the West seemed frozen. People speculated as to the reason of this inaction: the hopeful said that Joffre had a plan, that he was "nibbling"; others declared that we were short of munitions, others again that the new levies were not yet ripe for battle. So the months went by, and almost two years of war had been completed before the motionless English line began to stir and quiver as if it awoke from a long sleep, and began to roll onward, overwhelming the enemy.

The secret of the long inaction of the British armies has been well kept. On the one hand it was rigorously protected by the censorship, which, severe, and sometimes severe to the point of absurdity, became in this particular matter ferocious. As soon as the real significance of that which was happening was perceived by the authorities, an underlined circular was issued to the newspaper proprietors of Great Britain and Ireland. It warned each proprietor that he might impart the contents of this circular to one other person only, such person being the responsible editor of his paper, who was to keep the communication secret under the severest penalties. The circular forbade any mention of certain events that had taken place, that might take place; it forbade any kind of reference to these events or any hint of their existence. The subject was not to be referred to in conversation, it was not to be hinted at, however obscurely, in letters: the very existence of the circular, its subject apart, was to be a dead secret.

Now, a censorship that is sufficiently minute and utterly remorseless can do amazing things in the way of hiding what it wants to hide. Once one would have thought otherwise; one would have said that, censor or no censor, the fact of the murder at X—— would certainly become known, if not through the press, at all events through rumour and the passage of the news from mouth to mouth. And this would be true of England three hundred years ago. But we have grown of late to such a reverence for the printed word and such a reliance on it that the old faculty of disseminating news by word of mouth has become atrophied. Forbid the press to mention the fact that Jones has been murdered, and it is marvellous how few people will hear of it, and of those who hear how few will credit the story that they have heard.

And, then, again, the very fact of these vain rumours and fantastic tales having been so widely believed for a time was fatal to the credit of any stray mutterings that may have got abroad.

Before the secret circular had been issued my curiosity had somehow been aroused by certain paragraphs concerning a "Fatal Accident to Well-known Airman." The propeller of the airplane had been shattered, apparently by a collision with a flight of pigeons; the blades had been broken, and the machine had fallen like lead to the earth. And soon after I had seen this account, I heard of some very odd circumstances relating to an explosion in a great munition factory in the Midlands. I thought I saw the possibility of a connection between two very different events.

It has been pointed out to me by friends who have been good enough to read this record that certain phrases I have used may give the impression that I ascribe all the delays of the war on the Western front to the extraordinary circumstances which occasioned the issue of the secret circular. Of course this is not the case; there were many reasons for the immobility of our lines from October, 1914, to July, 1916. We could undertake to supply the defects of our army both in men and munitions *if* the new and incredible danger could be overcome. It has been overcome,—rather, perhaps, it has ceased to exist,—and the secret may now be told.

I have said my attention was attracted by an account of the death of a well-known airman. I have not the habit of preserving cuttings, I am sorry to say, so that I cannot be precise as to the date of this event. To the best of my belief it was either toward the end of May or the beginning of June, 1915. The manner in which Western-Reynolds met his death struck me as extraordinary. He was brought down by a flight of pigeons, as appeared by what was found on the blood-stained and shattered blades of the propeller. An eye-witness of the accident, a fellow-officer, described how Western-Reynolds set out from the aërodrome on a fine afternoon, there being hardly any wind. He was going to France.

" 'Wester' rose to a great height at once, and we could scarcely see the machine. I was turning to go when one of the fellows called out: 'I say! What's this?' He pointed up, and we saw what looked like a black cloud coming from the south at a tremendous rate. I saw at once it wasn't a cloud; it came with a swirl and a rush quite different from any cloud I've ever seen. It turned into a great crescent, and wheeled and veered about as if it was looking for something. The man who had called out had got his glasses, and was staring for all he was worth. Then he shouted that it was a tremendous flight of birds, 'thousands of them.' They went on wheeling and beating about high up in the air, and we were watching them, thinking it was interesting, but not supposing that they would make any difference to 'Wester,' who was just about out of sight. Then the two arms of the crescent drew in as quick as lightning, and these thousands of birds shot in a solid mass right up there across the sky, and flew away. Then Henley, the man with the glasses, called out, 'He's down!' and started running, and I went after him. We got a car, and as we were going along Henley told me that he'd seen the machine drop dead, as if it came out of that cloud of birds. We found the propeller-blades all broken and covered with blood and pigeon-feathers, and carcasses of the birds had got wedged in between the blades, and were sticking to them."

It was, I think, about a week or ten days after the airman's death that my business called me to a Northern town, the name of which, perhaps, had better remain unknown. My mission was to inquire into certain charges of extravagance which had been laid against the munition-workers of this special town. I found, as usual, that there was a mixture of truth and exaggeration in the stories that I had heard.

"And how can you be surprised if people will have a bit of a fling?" a worker said to me. "We're seeing money for the first time in our lives, and it's bright. And we work hard for it, and we risk our lives to get it. You've heard of explosion yonder?"

He mentioned certain works on the outskirts of the town. Of course neither the name of the works nor that of the town had been printed; there had been a brief notice of "Explosion at Munition Works in the Northern District: Many Fatalities." The working-man told me about it, and added some dreadful details.

"They wouldn't let their folks see bodies; screwed them up in coffins as they found them in shop. The gas had done it."

"Turned their faces black, you mean?"

"Nay. They were all as if they had been bitten to pieces."

This was a strange gas.

I asked the man in the Northern town all sorts of questions about the extraordinary explosion of which he had spoken to me, but he had very little more to say. As I have noted already, secrets that may not be printed are often deeply kept; last summer there were very few people outside high official circles who knew anything about the "tanks," of which we have all been talking lately, though these strange instruments of war were being exercised and tested in a park not far from London.

I gave him up, and took a tram to the district of the disaster, a sort of industrial suburb, five miles from the centre of the town. When I asked for the factory, I was told that it was no good my going to it, as there was nobody there. But I found it, a raw and hideous shed, with a walled yard about it, and a shut gate. I looked for signs of destruction, but there was nothing. The roof was quite undamaged; and again it struck me that this had been a strange accident. There had been an explosion of sufficient violence to kill people in the building, but the building itself showed no wounds or scars.

A man came out of the gate and locked it behind him. I began to ask him some sort of question, or, rather, I began to "open" for a question with "A terrible business here, they tell me," or some such phrase of convention. I got no further. The man asked me if I saw a policeman walking down the street.

I said I did, and I was given the choice of getting about my business forthwith or of being instantly given in charge as a spy. "Th' 'ast better be gone, and quick about it," was, I think, his final advice, and I took it.

It was a day or two later that the accident to the airman Western-Reynolds came into my mind. For one of those instants which are far shorter than any measure of time there flashed out the possibility of a link between the two disasters. But here was a wild impossibility, and I drove it away. And yet I think that the thought, mad as it seemed, never left me; it was the secret light that at last guided me through a sombre grove of enigmas.

It was about this time, so far as the date can be fixed, that a whole district, one might say a whole county, was visited by a series of extraordinary and terrible calamities, which were the more terrible inasmuch as they continued for some time to be inscrutable mysteries. It is indeed doubtful whether these awful events do not still remain mysteries to many of those concerned; for before the inhabitants of this part of the country had time to join one link of evidence to another the circular was issued, and thenceforth no one knew how to distinguish undoubted fact from wild and extravagant surmise.

The district in question is in the far west of Wales; I shall call it, for convenience, Meirion. Here, then, one sees a wild and divided and scattered region, a land of outland hills and secret and hidden valleys.

Such, then, in the main is Meirion, and on this land in the early summer of last year terror descended—a terror without shape, such as no man there had ever known.

It began with the tale of a little child who wandered out into the lanes to pick flowers one sunny afternoon, and never came back to the cottage on the hill. It was supposed that she must have crossed the road and gone to the cliff's edge, possibly in order to pick the sea-pinks that were then in full blossom. She must have slipped, they said, and fallen into the sea, two hundred feet below. It may be said at once that there was no doubt some truth in this conjecture, though it stopped far short of the whole truth. The child's body must have been carried out by the tide, for it was never found.

The conjecture of a false step or of a fatal slide on the slippery turf that slopes down to the rocks was accepted as being the only explanation possible. People thought the accident a strange one, because, as a rule, country children living by the cliffs and the sea become wary at an early age, and the little girl was almost ten years old. Still, as the neighbours said. "That's how it must have happened; and it's a great pity, to be sure." But this would not do when in a week's time a strong young labourer failed to come to his cottage after the day's work. His body was found on the rocks six or seven miles from the cliffs where the child was supposed to have fallen; he was going home by a path that he had used every night of his life for eight or nine years, that he used on dark nights in perfect security, knowing every inch of it. The police asked if he drank, but he was a teetotaller; if he was subject to fits, but he wasn't. And he was not murdered for his wealth, since agricultural labourers are not wealthy. It was only possible again to talk of slippery turf and a false step; but people began to be frightened. Then a woman was found with her neck broken at the bottom of a disused quarry near Llanfihangel, in the middle of the county. The false-step theory was eliminated here, for the quarry was guarded by a natural hedge of gorse. One would have to struggle and fight through sharp thorns to destruction in such a place as this; and indeed the gorse was broken, as if someone had rushed furiously through it, just above the place where the woman's body was found. And this also was strange: there was a dead sheep lying beside her in the pit, as if the woman and the sheep together had been chased over the brim of the quarry. But chased by whom or by what? And then there was a new form of terror.

This was in the region of the marshes under the mountain. A man and his son, a lad of fourteen or fifteen, set out early one morning to work, and never reached the farm whence they were bound. Their way skirted the marsh, but it was broad, firm, and well metalled, and it had been raised about two feet above the bog. But when search was made in the evening of the same day, Phillips and his son were found dead in the marsh, covered with black slime and pond-weed. And they lay some ten yards from the path, which, it would seem, they must have left deliberately. It was useless, of course, to look for tracks in the black ooze, for if one threw a big stone into it, a few seconds removed all marks of the disturbance. The men who found the two bodies beat about the verges and purlieus of the marsh in hope of finding some trace of the murderers; they went to and fro over the rising ground where the black cattle were grazing, they searched the alder-thickets by the brook: but they discovered nothing.

Most horrible of all these horrors, perhaps, was the affair of the Highway, a lonely and unfrequented by-road that winds for many miles on high and lonely land. Here, a mile from any other dwelling, stands a cottage on the edge of a dark wood. It was inhabited by a labourer named Williams, his wife, and their three children. One hot summer's evening a man who had been doing a day's gardening at a rectory three or four miles away passed the cottage, and stopped for a few minutes to chat with Williams, who was pottering about his garden, while the children were playing on the path by the door. The two talked of their neighbours and of the potatoes till Mrs. Williams appeared at the doorway and said supper was ready, and Williams turned to go into the house. This was about eight o'clock, and in the ordinary course the family would have had their supper and be in bed by nine, or by half-past nine at the latest.

At ten o'clock that night the local doctor was driving home along the Highway. His horse shied violently and then stopped dead just opposite the gate to the cottage. The doctor got down, and there on the roadway lay Williams, his wife, and the three children, stone-dead. Their skulls were battered in as if by some heavy iron instrument; their faces were beaten into a pulp.

It is not easy to make any picture of the horror that lay dark on the hearts of the people of Meirion. It was no longer possible to believe or to pretend to believe that these men and women and children had met their deaths through strange accidents. For a time people said that there must be a madman at large, a sort of country variant of Jack the Ripper, some horrible pervert who was possessed by the passion of death, who prowled darkling about that lonely land, hiding in woods and in wild places, always watching and seeking for the victims of his desire.

Indeed, Dr. Lewis, who found poor Williams, his wife, and children, was convinced at first that the presence of a concealed madman in the country-side offered the only possible solution to the difficulty.

"I felt sure," he said to me afterward, "that the Williamses had been killed by a homicidal maniac. It was the nature of the poor creatures' injuries that convinced me that this was the case. Those poor people had their heads smashed to pieces by what must have been a storm of blows. Any one of them would have been fatal, but the murderer must have gone on raining blows with his iron hammer on people who were already stone-dead. And *that* sort of thing is the work of a madman, and nothing but a madman. That's how I argued the matter out to myself just after the event. I was utterly wrong, monstrously wrong; but who could have suspected the truth?"

I quote Dr. Lewis, or the substance of him, as representative of most of the educated opinion of the district at the beginnings of the terror. People seized on this theory largely because it offered at least the comfort of an explanation, and any explanation, even the poorest, is better than an intolerable and terrible mystery. Besides, Dr. Lewis's theory was plausible: it explained the lack of purpose that seemed to characterise the murders.

And yet there were difficulties even from the first. It was hardly possible that a strange madman would be able to keep hidden in a country-side where any stranger is instantly noted and noticed; sooner or later he would be seen as he prowled along the lanes or across the wild places.

Then another theory, or, rather, a variant of Dr. Lewis's theory, was started. This was to the effect that the person responsible for the outrages was indeed a madman, but a madman only at intervals. It was one of the members of the Porth Club, a certain Mr. Remnant, who was supposed to have originated this more subtle explanation. Mr. Remnant was a middle-aged man who, having nothing particular to do, read a great many books by way of conquering the hours. He talked to the club—doctors, retired colonels, parsons, lawyers—about "personality," quoted various psychological text-books in support of his contention that personality was sometimes fluid and unstable, went back to "Dr. Jekyll and Mr. Hyde" as good evidence of this proposition, and laid stress on *Dr. Jekyll's* speculation that the human soul, so far from being one and indivisible, might possibly turn out to be a mere polity, a state in which dwelt many strange and incongruous citizens, whose characters were not merely unknown, but altogether unsurmised by that form of consciousness which rashly assumed that it was not only the president of the republic, but also its sole citizen.

However, Mr. Remnant's somewhat crazy theory became untenable when two more victims of an awful and mysterious death were offered up in sacrifice, for a man was found dead in the Llanfihangel quarry where the woman had been discovered, and on the same day a girl of fifteen was found broken on the jagged rocks under the cliffs near Porth. Now, it appeared that these two deaths must have occurred at about the same time, within an hour of one another, certainly, and the distance between the quarry and the cliffs by Black Rock is certainly twenty miles.

And now a fresh circumstance or set of circumstances became manifest to confound judgment and to awaken new and wild surmises; for at about this time people realized that none of the dreadful events that were happening all about them was so much as mentioned in the press. Horror followed on horror, but no word was printed in any of the local journals. The curious went to the newspaper offices—there were two left in the county,—but found nothing save a firm refusal to discuss the matter. Then the Cardiff papers were drawn and found blank, and the London press was apparently ignorant of the fact that crimes that had no parallel were terrorising a whole country-side. Everybody wondered what could have happened, what was happening; and then it was whispered that the coroner would allow no inquiry to be made as to these deaths of darkness.

Clearly, people reasoned, these government restrictions and prohibitions could only refer to the war, to some great danger in connection with the war. And that being so, it followed that the outrages which must be kept so secret were the work of the enemy; that is, of concealed German agents.

It is time, I think, for me to make one point clear. I began this history with certain references to an extraordinary accident to an airman whose machine fell to the ground after collision with a huge flock of pigeons, and then to an explosion in a Northern munition factory of a very singular kind. Then I deserted the neighbourhood of London and the Northern district, and dwelt on a mysterious and terrible series of events which occurred in the summer of 1915 in a Welsh county, which I have named for convenience Meirion.

Well, let it be understood at once that all this detail that I have given about the occurrences in Meirion does not imply that the county in Wales was alone or specially afflicted by the terror that was over the land. They tell me that in the villages about Dartmoor the stout Devonshire hearts sank as men's hearts used to sink in the time of plague and pestilence. There was horror, too, about the Norfolk Broads, and far up by Perth no one would venture on the path that leads by Scone to the wooded heights above the Tay. And in the industrial districts. I met a man by chance one day in an odd London corner who spoke with horror of what a friend had told him.

" 'Ask no questions, Ned,' he says to me, 'but I tell yow a was in Bairnigan t' other day, and a met a pal who'd seen three hundred coffins going out of a works not far from there.' "

Then there was the vessel that hovered outside the mouth of the Thames with all sails set, and beat to and fro in the wind, and never answered any signals and showed no light. The forts shot at her, and brought down one of the masts; but she went suddenly about, stood down channel, and drove ashore at last on the sand-banks and pine-woods of Arcachon, and not a man alive on her, but only rattling heaps of bones! That last voyage of the *Semiramis* would be something horribly worth telling; but I heard it only at a distance as a yarn, and believed it only because it squared with other things that I knew for certain.

This, then, is my point: I have written of the terror as it fell on Meirion simply because I have had opportunities of getting close there to what really happened.

Well, I have said that the people of that far Western county realized not only that death was abroad in their quiet lanes and on their peaceful hills, but that for some reason it was to be kept secret. And so they concluded that this veil of secrecy must somehow be connected with the war; and from this position it was not a long way to a further inference that the murderers of innocent men and women and children were either Germans or agents of Germany. It would be just like the Huns, everybody agreed, to think out such a devilish scheme as this; and they always thought out their schemes beforehand.

It all seemed plausible enough; Germany had by this time perpetrated so many horrors and had so excelled in devil-ish ingenuities that no abomination seemed too abominable to be probable or too ingeniously wicked to be beyond her tortuous malice. But then came the questions as to who the agents of this terrible design were, as to where they lived, as to how they contrived to move unseen from field to field, from lane to lane. All sorts of fantastic attempts were made to answer these questions, but it was felt that they remained unanswered. Some suggested that the murderers landed from submarines, or flew from hiding-places on the west coast of Ireland, coming and going by night; but there were seen to be flagrant impossibilities in both these suggestions. Everybody agreed that the evil work was no doubt the work of Germany; but nobody could begin to guess how it was done.

It was, I suppose, at about this time when the people were puzzling their heads as to the secret methods used by the Ger-mans or their agents to accomplish their crimes that a very singular circumstance became known to a few of the Porth people. It related to the murder of the Williams family on the Highway in front of their cottage door. I do not know that I have made it plain that the old Roman road called the High-way follows the course of a long, steep hill that goes steadily westward till it slants down toward the sea. On each side of the road the ground falls away, here into deep shadowy woods, here into high pastures, but for the most part into the wild and broken land that is characteristic of Arfon.

Now, on the lower slopes of it, beneath the Williams cot-tage, some three or four fields down the hill, there is a military camp. The place has been used as a camp for many years, and lately the site has been extended and huts have been erected;

but a considerable number of the men were under canvas here
in the summer of 1915.

On the night of the Highway murder this camp, as it
appeared afterward, was the scene of the extraordinary panic
of horses.

A good many men in the camp were asleep in their tents
soon after 9:30. They woke up in panic. There was a thundering sound on the steep hillside above them, and down upon
the tents came half a dozen horses, mad with fright, trampling
the canvas, trampling the men, bruising dozens of them, and
killing two.

Everything was in wild confusion, men groaning and
screaming in the darkness, struggling with the canvas and the
twisted ropes, and some of them, raw lads enough, shouting
out that the Germans had at last landed.

Some of the men had seen the horses galloping down the
hill as if terror itself was driving them. They scattered off into
the darkness, and somehow or other found their way back in
the night to their pasture above the camp. They were grazing
there peacefully in the morning, and the only sign of the panic
of the night before was the mud they had scattered all over
themselves as they pelted through a patch of wet ground. The
farmer said they were as quiet a lot as any in Meirion; he could
make nothing of it.

Then two or three other incidents, quite as odd and incomprehensible, came to be known, borne on chance trickles of
gossip that came into the towns from outland farms. And in
such ways it came out that up at Plas Newydd there had been
a terrible business over swarming the bees; they had turned as
wild as wasps and much more savage. They had come about the
people who were taking the swarms like a cloud. They settled
on one man's face so that you could not see the flesh for the
bees crawling over it, and they had stung him so badly that
the doctor did not know whether he would get well; they had

chased a girl who had come out to see the swarming, and settled on her and stung her to death. Then they had gone off to a brake below the farm and got into a hollow tree, and it was not safe to go near it, for they would come out at you by day or by night.

And much the same thing had happened, it seemed, at three or four farms and cottages where bees were kept. And there were stories, hardly so clear or so credible, of sheep-dogs, mild and trusted beasts, turning as savage as wolves and injuring the farm boys in a horrible manner, in one case, it was said, with fatal results. It was certainly true that old Mrs. Owens's favourite Dorking cock had gone mad. She came into Porth one Saturday morning with her face and her neck all bound up and plastered. She had gone out to her bit of field to feed the poultry the night before, and the bird had flown at her and attacked her most savagely, inflicting some very nasty wounds before she could beat it off.

"There was a stake handy, lucky for me," she said, "and I did beat him and beat him till the life was out of him. But what is come to the world, whatever?"

Now Remnant, the man of theories, was also a man of extreme leisure. He was no more brutal than the general public, which revels in the details of mysterious crime; but it must be said that the terror, black though it was, was a boon to him. He peered and investigated and poked about with the relish of a man to whose life a new zest has been added. He listened attentively to the strange tales of bees and dogs and poultry that came into Porth with the country baskets of butter, rabbits, and green peas, and he evolved at last a most extraordinary theory. He went one night to see Dr. Lewis.

"I want to talk to you," he said to the doctor, "about what I have called provisionally the Z-ray."

Dr. Lewis, smiling indulgently, and quite prepared for some monstrous piece of theorising, led Remnant into the room that overlooked the terraced garden and the sea.

"I suppose, Lewis, you've heard these extraordinary stories of bees and dogs and things that have been going about lately?"

"Certainly I have heard them. I was called in at Plas Newydd, and treated Thomas Trevor, who's only just out of danger, by the way. I certified for the poor child, Mary Trevor. She was dying when I got to the place."

"Well, then there are the stories of good-tempered old sheep-dogs turning wicked and 'savaging' children."

"Quite so. I haven't seen any of these cases professionally; but I believe the stories are accurate enough."

"And the old woman assaulted by her own poultry?"

"That's perfectly true."

"Very good," said Mr. Remnant. He spoke now with an italic impressiveness, *"Don't you see the link between all this and the horrible things that have been happening about here for the last month?"*

Lewis stared at Remnant in amazement. He lifted his red eyebrows and lowered them in a kind of scowl. His speech showed traces of his native accent.

"Great burning!" he exclaimed, "what on earth are you getting at now? It is madness. Do you mean to tell me that you think there is some connection between a swarm or two of bees that have turned nasty, a cross dog, and a wicked old barn-door cock, and these poor people that have been pitched over the cliffs and hammered to death on the road? There's no sense in it, you know."

"I am strongly inclined to believe that there is a great deal of sense in it," replied Remnant, with extreme calmness. "Look here, Lewis, I saw you grinning the other day at the club when I was telling the fellows that in my opinion all these outrages had been committed, certainly by the Germans, but by some method of which we have no conception. Do you see my point?"

"Well, in a sort of way. You mean there's an absolute originality in the method? I suppose that is so. But what next?"

Remnant seemed to hesitate, partly from a sense of the portentous nature of what he was about to say, partly from a sort of half-unwillingness to part with so profound a secret.

"Well," he said, "you will allow that we have two sets of phenomena of a very extraordinary kind occurring at the same time. Don't you think that it's only reasonable to connect the two sets with one another?"

"So the philosopher of Tenterden steeple and the Goodwin Sands[1] thought, certainly," said Lewis. "But what is the connection? Those poor folks on the Highway weren't stung by bees or worried by a dog. And horses don't throw people over cliffs or stifle them in marshes."

"No; I never meant to suggest anything so absurd. It is evident to me that in all these cases of animals turning suddenly savage the cause has been terror, panic, fear. The horses that went charging into the camp were mad with fright, we know. And I say that in the other instances we have been discussing the cause was the same. The creatures were exposed to an infection of fear, and a frightened beast or bird or insect uses its weapons, whatever they may be. If, for example, there had been anybody with those horses when they took their panic, they would have lashed out at him with their heels."

"Yes, I dare say that that is so. Well?" demanded the doctor.

---

1 Goodwin Sands and the town of Tenterden are in Kent, UK. The saying, "Tenterden steeple was the cause of Goodwin Sands" was formerly used as a satirical riposte when an absurd cause was proposed for something. While the saying is an apparent non sequitur, the original story holds that the Abbot of St Augustine, Canterbury, used funds intended for the maintenance of the seawall protecting Earl Godwin's Island to build Tenterden steeple; the seawall was thus breached, and the resulting inundation in the year 1099 created Goodwin Sands.

"Well, my belief is that the Germans have made an extraordinary discovery. I have called it the Z-ray. You know that the ether is merely an hypothesis; we have to suppose that it's there to account for the passage of the Marconi current from one place to another. Now, suppose that there is a psychic ether as well as a material ether, suppose that it is possible to direct irresistible impulses across this medium, suppose that these impulses are toward murder or suicide; then I think that you have an explanation of the terrible series of events that have been happening in Meirion for the last few weeks. And it is quite clear to my mind that the horses and the other creatures have been exposed to this Z-ray, and that it has produced on them the effect of terror, with ferocity as the result of terror. Now, what do you say to that? Telepathy, you know, is well established; so is hypnotic suggestion. Now don't you feel that putting telepathy and suggestion together, as it were, you have more than the elements of what I call the Z-ray? I feel that I have more to go on in making my hypothesis than the inventor of the steam-engine had in making his hypothesis when he saw the lid of the kettle bobbing up and down. What do you say?"

Dr. Lewis made no answer. He was watching the growth of a new, unknown tree in his garden.

It was a dark summer night. The moon was old and faint above the Dragon's Head, on the opposite side of the bay, and the air was very still. It was so still that Lewis had noted that not a leaf stirred on the very tip of a high tree that stood out against the sky; and yet he knew that he was listening to some sound that he could not determine or define. It was not the wind in the leaves, it was not the gentle wash of the water of the sea against the rocks; that latter sound he could distinguish easily. But there was something else. It was scarcely a sound; it was as if the air itself trembled and fluttered, as the air trembles in a church when they open the great pedal pipes of the organ.

The doctor listened intently. It was not an illusion, the sound was not in his own head, as he had suspected for a moment; but for the life of him he could not make out whence it came or what it was. He gazed down into the night, over the terraces of his garden, now sweet with the scent of the flowers of the night; tried to peer over the tree-tops across the sea toward the Dragon's Head. It struck him suddenly that this strange, fluttering vibration of the air might be the noise of a distant aëroplane or airship; there was not the usual droning hum, but this sound might be caused by a new type of engine. A new type of engine? Possibly it was an enemy airship; their range, it had been said, was getting longer, and Lewis was just going to call Remnant's attention to the sound, to its possible cause, and to the possible danger that might be hovering over them, when he saw something that caught his breath and his heart with wild amazement and a touch of terror.

He had been staring upward into the sky, and, about to speak to Remnant, he had let his eyes drop for an instant. He looked down toward the trees in the garden, and saw with utter astonishment that one had changed its shape in the few hours that had passed since the setting of the sun. There was a thick grove of ilexes bordering the lowest terrace, and above them rose one tall pine, spreading its head of sparse branches dark against the sky.

As Lewis glanced down over the terraces he saw that the tall pine-tree was no longer there. In its place there rose above the ilexes what might have been a greater ilex; there was the blackness of a dense growth of foliage rising like a broad, far-spreading, and rounded cloud over the lesser trees.

Dr. Lewis glared into the dimness of the night, at the great, spreading tree that he knew could not be there. And as he gazed he saw that what at first appeared the dense blackness of foliage was fretted and starred with wonderful appearances of lights and colours.

The night had gloomed over; clouds obscured the faint moon and the misty stars. Lewis rose, with some kind of warning and inhibiting gesture to Remnant, who, he was aware, was gaping at him in astonishment. He walked to the open French window, took a pace forward on the path outside, and looked very intently at the dark shape of the tree. He shaded the light of the lamp behind him by holding his hands on each side of his eyes.

The mass of the tree—the tree that couldn't be there—stood out against the sky, but not so clearly now that the clouds had rolled up. Its edges, the limits of its leafage, were not so distinct. Lewis thought that he could detect some sort of quivering movement in it, though the air was at a dead calm. It was a night on which one might hold up a lighted match and watch it burn without any wavering or inclination of the flame.

"You know," said Lewis, "how a bit of burned paper will sometimes hang over the coals before it goes up the chimney, and little worms of fire will shoot through it. It was like that, if you should be standing some distance away. Just threads and hairs of yellow light I saw, and specks and sparks of fire, and then a twinkling of a ruby no bigger than a pin-point, and a green wandering in the black, as if an emerald were crawling, and then little veins of deep blue. 'Woe is me!' I said to myself in Welsh. 'What is all this colour and burning?'

"At that very moment there came a thundering rap at the door of the room inside, and there was my man telling me that I was wanted directly up at the Garth, as old Mr. Trevor Williams had been taken very bad. I knew his heart was not worth much, so I had to go off directly, and leave Remnant alone to make what he could of it all."

Dr. Lewis was kept some time at the Garth. It was past twelve when he got back to his house. He went quickly to the room that overlooked the garden and the sea, threw open the French window, and peered into the darkness. There, dim indeed against the dim sky, but unmistakable, was the tall pine, with its sparse branches, high above the dense growth of the ilex-trees. The strange boughs which had amazed him had vanished; there was no appearance of colours or of fires.

The doctor did not say anything about the strange tree to Remnant. When they next met, he said that he had thought there was a man hiding among the bushes. This was in explanation of that warning gesture he had used, and of his going out into the garden and staring into the night. He concealed the truth because he dreaded the Remnant doctrine that would undoubtedly be produced; indeed, he hoped that he had heard the last of the theory of the Z-ray. But Remnant firmly reopened this subject.

"We were interrupted just as I was putting my case to you," he said. "And to sum it all up, it amounts to this: the Huns have made one of the great leaps of science. They are sending 'suggestions' (which amount to irresistible commands) over here, and the persons affected are seized with suicidal or homicidal mania. In my opinion Evans was the murderer of the Williams family. You know he said he stopped to talk to Williams. It seems to me simple. And as for the animals,— the horses, dogs, and so forth,—they, as I say, were no doubt panic-stricken by the ray, and hence driven to frenzy."

"Why should Evans have murdered Williams instead of Williams murdering Evans? Why should the impact of the ray affect one and not the other?"

"Why does one man react violently to a certain drug, while it makes no impression on another man? Why is A able to drink a bottle of whisky and remain sober, while B is turned into something very like a lunatic after he has drunk three glasses?"

"It is a question of idiosyncrasy," said the doctor.

Lewis escaped from the club and from Remnant. He did not want to hear any more about that dreadful ray, because he felt sure that the ray was all nonsense. But asking himself why he felt this certitude in the matter, he had to confess that he didn't know. An aëroplane, he reflected, was all nonsense before it was made.

But he thought with fervour of the extraordinary thing he had seen in his own garden with his own eyes. How could one fail to be afraid with great amazement at the thought of such a mystery?

Dr. Lewis's thoughts were distracted from the incredible adventure of the tree by the visit of his sister and her husband. Mr. and Mrs. Merritt lived in a well-known manufacturing town of the Midlands, which was now, of course, a centre of munition work. On the day of their arrival at Porth, Mrs. Merritt, who was tired after the long, hot journey, went to bed early, and Merritt and Lewis went into the room by the garden for their talk and tobacco. They spoke of the year that had passed since their last meeting, of the weary dragging of the war, of friends that had perished in it, of the hopelessness of an early ending of all this misery. Lewis said nothing of the terror that was on the land. One does not greet with a tale of horror a tired man who is come to a quiet, sunny place for relief from black smoke and work and worry. Indeed, the doctor saw that his brother-in-law looked far from well. He seemed "jumpy"; there was an occasional twitch of his mouth that Lewis did not like at all.

"Well," said the doctor, after an interval of silence and port wine, "I am glad to see you here again. Porth always suits you. I don't think you're looking quite up to your usual form; but three weeks of Meirion air will do wonders."

"Well, I hope it will," said the other. "I am not up to the mark. Things are not going well at Midlingham."

"Business is all right, isn't it?"

"Yes; but there are other things that are all wrong. We are living under a reign of terror. It comes to that."

"What on earth do you mean?"

"It's not much. I didn't dare write it. But do you know that at every one of the munition-works in Midlingham and all about it there's a guard of soldiers with drawn bayonets and loaded rifles day and night? Men with bombs, too. And machine-guns at the big factories."

"German spies?"

"You don't want machine-guns and bombs to fight spies with."

"But what against?"

"Nobody knows. Nobody knows what is happening," Merritt repeated, and he went on to describe the bewilderment and terror that hung like a cloud over the great industrial city in the Midlands; how the feeling of concealment, or some intolerable secret danger that must not be named, was worst of all.

Merritt made a sort of picture of the great town cowering in its fear of an unknown danger.

"There's a queer story going about," he said, "as to a place right out in the country, over the other side of Midlingham. They've built one of the new factories out there, a great red brick town of sheds. About two hundred yards from this place there's an old footpath through a pretty large wood, most of it thick undergrowth. It's a black place of nights.

"A man had to go this way one night. He got along all right till he came to the wood, and then he said his heart dropped out of his body. It was awful to hear the noises in that wood. Thousands of men were in it, he swears. It was full of rustling, and pattering of feet trying to go dainty, and the crack of dead boughs lying on the ground as someone trod on them, and swishing of the grass, and some sort of chattering speech going on that sounded, so he said, as if the dead sat in their bones and talked! He ran for his life, anyhow, across fields, over hedges, through brooks. He must have run, by his tale, ten miles out of his way before he got home to his wife, beat at the door, broke in, and bolted it behind him."

"There is something rather alarming about any wood at night," said Dr. Lewis.

Merritt shrugged his shoulders.

"People say that the Germans have landed, and that they are hiding in underground places all over the country."

Lewis gasped for a moment, silent in contemplation of the magnificence of rumour. The Germans already landed, hiding underground, striking by night, secretly, terribly, at the power of England! It was monstrous, and yet—

"People say they've got a new kind of poison-gas," continued Merritt. "Some think that they dig underground places and make the gas there, and lead it by secret pipes into the shops; others say that they throw gas bombs into the factories. It must be worse than anything they've used in France, from what the authorities say."

"The authorities? Do *they* admit that there are Germans in hiding about Midlingham?"

"No. They call it 'explosions.' But we know it isn't explosions. We know in the Midlands what an explosion sounds like and looks like. And we know that the people killed in these 'explosions' are put into their coffins in the works. Their own relations are not allowed to see them."

"And do you believe in the German theory?"

"If I do, it's because one must believe in something. Some say they've seen the gas. I heard that a man living in Dunwich saw it one night like a black cloud, with sparks of fire in it, floating over the tops of the trees by Dunwich Common."

The light of an ineffable amazement came into Lewis's eyes. The night of Remnant's visit, the trembling vibration of the air, the dark tree that had grown in his garden since the setting of the sun, the strange leafage that was starred with burning, and all vanished away when he returned from his visit to the Garth; and such a leafage had appeared as a burning cloud far in the heart of England. What intolerable mystery, what tremendous doom was signified in this? But one thing was clear and certain: the terror of Meirion was also the terror of the Midlands.

Merritt told the story of how a Swedish professor, Huvelius, had sold to the Germans a plan for filling England with German soldiers. Land was to be bought in certain suitable and well-considered places, Englishmen were to be bought as the apparent owners of such land, and secret excavations were to be made, till the country was literally undermined. A subterranean Germany, in fact, was to be dug under selected districts of England; there were to be great caverns, underground cities, well drained, well ventilated, supplied with water, and in these places vast stores both of food and of munitions were to be accumulated year after year till "the Day" dawned. And then, warned in time, the secret garrison would leave shops, hotels, offices, villas, and vanish underground, ready to begin their work of bleeding England at the heart.

"Well," said Lewis, "of course, it may be so. If it is so, it is terrible beyond words."

Indeed, he found something horribly plausible in the story. It was an extraordinary plan, of course, an unheard-of scheme; but it did not seem impossible. It was the Trojan Horse on a gigantic scale. And this theory certainly squared with what one had heard of German preparations in Belgium and in France.

And it seemed from that wonder of the burning tree that the enemy mysteriously and terribly present at Midlingham was present also in Meirion. Yet, he thought again, there was but little harm to be done in Meirion to the armies of England or to their munitionment. They were working for panic terror. Possibly that might be so; but the camp under the Highway? That should be their first object, and no harm had been done there.

Lewis did not know that since the panic of the horses men had died terribly in that camp; that it was now a fortified place, with a deep, broad trench, a thick tangle of savage barbed wire about it, and a machine-gun planted at each corner.

One evening the doctor was summoned to a little hamlet on the outskirts of Porth. In one of the cottages the doctor found a father and mother weeping and crying out to "Doctor Bach, Doctor Bach," two frightened children, and one little body, still and dead.

The doctor found that the child had been asphyxiated. His clothes were dry; it was not a case of drowning. There was no mark of strangling. He asked the father how it had happened, and father and mother, weeping most lamentably, declared they had no knowledge of how their child had been killed, "unless it was the People that had done it." The Celtic fairies are still malignant. Lewis asked what had happened that evening; where had the child been?

"Was he with his brother and sister?" asked the doctor. "Don't they know anything about it?"

The children had been playing in the road at dusk, and just as their mother called them in one child had heard Johnnie cry out:

"Oh, what is that beautiful, shiny thing over the stile?"

They found the little body, under the ash-grove in the middle of the field. He was quite still and dead, so still that a great moth had settled on his forehead, fluttering away when they lifted him up.

Dr. Lewis heard this story. There was nothing to be done, little to be said to these most unhappy people.

"Take care of the two that you have left to you," said the doctor as he went away. "Don't let them out of your sight if you can help it. It is dreadful times that we are living in."

About ten days later a young farmer had been found by his wife lying in the grass close to the castle, with no scar on him or any mark of violence, but stone-dead.

Lewis was sent for, and knew at once, when he saw the dead man, that he had perished in the way that the little boy had perished, whatever that awful way might be.

It seemed that he had gone out at about half-past nine to look after some beasts. He told his wife he would be back in a quarter of an hour or twenty minutes. He did not return, and when he had been gone for three quarters of an hour Mrs. Cradock went out to look for him. She went into the field where the beasts were, and everything seemed all right; but there was no trace of Cradock. She called out; there was no answer.

She told the doctor:

"There was something that I could not make out at all. It seemed to me that the hedge did look different from usual. To be sure, things do look different at night, and there was a bit of sea mist about; but somehow it did look odd to me, and I said to myself, 'Have I lost my way, then?' "

She declared that the shape of the trees in the hedge appeared to have changed, and besides, it had a look "as if it was lighted up, somehow," and so she went on toward the stile to see what all this could be; and when she came near, everything was as usual. She looked over the stile and called, hoping to see her husband coming toward her or to hear his voice; but there was no answer, and glancing down the path, she saw, or thought she saw, some sort of brightness on the ground, "a dim sort of light, like a bunch of glow-worms in a hedge-bank.

"And so I climbed over the stile and went down the path, and the light seemed to melt away; and there was my poor husband lying on his back, saying not a word to me when I spoke to him and touched him."

So for Lewis the terror blackened and became altogether intolerable, and others, he perceived, felt as he did. He did not know, he never asked, whether the men at the club had heard of these deaths of the child and the young farmer; but no one spoke of them. Indeed, the change was evident; at the beginning of the terror men spoke of nothing else; now it had become all too awful for ingenious chatter or laboured and grotesque theories. And Lewis had received a letter from his brother-in-law, who had gone back to Midlingham; it contained the sentence, "I am afraid Fanny's health has not greatly benefitted by her visit to Porth; there are still several symptoms I don't at all like." This told him, in a phraseology that the doctor and Merritt had agreed upon, that the terror remained heavy in the Midland town.

It was soon after the death of Cradock that people began to tell strange tales of a sound that was to be heard of nights about the hills and valleys to the northward of Porth. A man who had missed the last train from Meiros and had been forced to tramp the ten miles between Meiros and Porth seems to have been the first to hear it. He said he had got to the top of the hill by Tredonoc, somewhere between half-past ten and eleven, when he first noticed an odd noise that he could not make out at all; it was like a shout, a long-drawn-out, dismal wail coming from a great way off. He stopped to listen, thinking at first that it might be owls hooting in the woods; but it was different, he said, from that. He could make nothing of it, and feeling frightened, he did not quite know of what, he walked on briskly, and was glad to see the lights of Porth station. Then others heard it.

Let it be remembered again and again that all the while that the terror lasted there was no common stock of information as to the dreadful things that were being done. The press had not said one word upon it, there was no criterion by which the mass of the people could separate fact from mere vague rumour, no test by which ordinary misadventure or disaster could be distinguished from the achievements of the secret and awful force that was at work. And since the real nature of all this mystery of death was unknown, it followed easily that the signs and warnings and omens of it were all the more unknown. Here was horror, there was horror; but there were no links to join one horror with another, no common basis of knowledge from which the connection between this horror and that horror might be inferred.

The sound had been heard for three or perhaps four nights, when the people coming out of Tredonoc church after morning service on Sunday noticed that there was a big yellow sheep-dog in the churchyard. The dog, it appeared, had been waiting for the congregation; for it at once attached itself to them, at first to the whole body, and then to a group of half a dozen who took the turning to the right till they came to a gate in the hedge, whence a roughly made farm-road went through the fields, and dipped down into the woods and to Treff Loyne farm.

Then the dog became like a possessed creature. He barked furiously. He ran up to one of the men and looked up at him, "as if he were begging for his life," as the man said, and then rushed to the gate and stood by it, wagging his tail and barking at intervals. The men stared.

"Whose dog will that be?" said one of them.

"It will be Thomas Griffith's, Treff Loyne," said another.

"Well, then, why doesn't he go home? Go home, then!" He went through the gesture of picking up a stone from the road and throwing it at the dog. "Go home, then! Over the gate with you!"

But the dog never stirred. He barked and whined and ran up to the men and then back to the gate. The farmer shook the dog off, and the four went on their way, and the dog stood in the road and watched them, and then put up its head and uttered a long and dismal howl that was despair.

Then it occurred to somebody, so far as I can make out with no particular reference to the odd conduct of the Treff Loyne sheep-dog, that Thomas Griffith had not been seen for some time past.

One September afternoon, therefore, a party went up to discover what had happened to Griffith and his family. There were half a dozen farmers, a couple of policemen, and four soldiers, carrying their arms; those last had been lent by the officer commanding at the camp. Lewis, too, was of the party;

he had heard by chance that no one knew what had become of Griffith and his family, and he was anxious about a young fellow, a painter, of his acquaintance who had been lodging at Treff Loyne all the summer.

They came to the gate in the hedge where the farm-road led down to Treff Loyne. Here was the farm inclosure, the outlying walls of the yard and the barns and sheds and outhouses. One of the farmers threw open the gate and walked into the yard, and forthwith began bellowing at the top of his voice:

"Thomas Griffith! Thomas Griffith! Where be you, Thomas Griffith?"

The rest followed him. The corporal snapped out an order over his shoulder, and there was a rattling metallic noise as the men fixed their bayonets.

There was no answer to this summons; but they found poor Griffith lying on his face at the edge of the pond in the middle of the yard. There was a ghastly wound in his side, as if a sharp stake had been driven into his body.

It was a still September afternoon. No wind stirred in the hanging woods that were dark all about the ancient house of Treff Loyne; the only sound in the dim air was the lowing of the cattle. They had wandered, it seemed, from the fields and had come in by the gate of the farm-yard and stood there melancholy, as if they mourned for their dead master. And the horses, four great, heavy, patient-looking beasts, were there, too, and in the lower field the sheep were standing, as if they waited to be fed.

Lewis knelt down by the dead man and looked closely at the gaping wound in his side.

"He's been dead a long time," he said. "How about the family? How many are there of them? I never attended them."

"There was Griffith, and his wife, his son Thomas, and Mary Griffith, his daughter. And I do think there was a gentleman lodging with them this summer."

That was from one of the farmers. They all looked at one another, this party of rescue, who knew nothing of the danger that had smitten this house of quiet people, nothing of the peril which had brought them to this pass of a farm-yard, with a dead man in it, and his beasts standing patiently about him as if they waited for the farmer to rise up and give them their food. Then the party turned to the house. The windows were shut tight. There was no sign of any life or movement about the place. The party of men looked at one another.

They did not know what the danger was or where it might strike them or whether it was from without or from within. They stared at the murdered man, and gazed dismally at one another.

"Come," said Lewis, "we must do something. We must get into the house, and see what is wrong."

"Yes, but suppose they are at us while we are getting in?" said the sergeant. "Where shall we be then, Doctor Lewis?"

The corporal put one of his men by the gate at the top of the farm-yard, another at the gate by the bottom, and told them to challenge and shoot. The doctor and the rest opened the little gate of the front garden and went up to the porch and stood listening by the door. It was all dead silence. Lewis took an ash stick from one of the farmers and beat heavily three times on the old, black, oaken door studded with antique nails.

There was no answer from within. He beat again, and still silence. He shouted to the people within, but there was no answer. They all turned and looked at one another. There was an iron ring on the door. Lewis turned it, but the door stood fast; it was evidently barred and bolted. The sergeant of police called out to open, but again there was no answer.

They consulted together. There was nothing for it but to blow the door open, and some one of them called in a loud voice to those that might be within to stand away from the door or they would be killed. And at this very moment the yellow sheep-dog came bounding up the yard from the woods and licked their hands and fawned on them and barked joyfully.

"Indeed, now," said one of the farmers, "he did know that there was something amiss. A pity it was, Thomas Williams, that we did not follow him when he implored us last Sunday."

The corporal disengaged his bayonet and shot into the keyhole, calling out once more before he fired. He shot and shot again, so heavy and firm was the ancient door, so stout its bolts and fastenings. At last he had to fire at the massive hinges, and then they all pushed together, and at that the door lurched open suddenly and fell forward.

Young Griffith was lying dead before the hearth. They went on toward the parlour, and in the doorway of the room was the body of the artist Secretan, as if he had fallen in trying to get to the kitchen. Up-stairs the two women, Mrs. Griffith and her daughter, a girl of eighteen, were lying together on the bed in the big bedroom, clasped in each other's arms.

They went about the house, searched the pantries, the back kitchen, and the cellars; there was no life in it. There was no bread in the place, no milk, no water.

The group of men stood in the big kitchen and stared at one another, a dreadful perplexity in their eyes. The old man had been killed with the piercing thrust of some sharp weapon; the rest had perished, it seemed probable, of thirst; but what possible enemy was this that besieged the farm and shut in its inhabitants? There was no answer.

The sergeant of police spoke of getting a cart and taking the bodies into Porth, and Dr. Lewis went into the parlour that Secretan had used as a sitting-room, intending to gather any possessions or effects of the dead artist that he might possibly find there. Half a dozen portfolios were piled up in one corner, there were some books on a side-table, a fishing-rod and basket behind the door; that seemed all. Lewis was about to rejoin the rest of the party in the kitchen, when he looked down at some scattered papers lying with the books on the side-table. On one of the sheets he read, to his astonishment, the words, "Dr. James Lewis, Porth." This was written in a staggering, trembling scrawl.

The table stood in a dark corner of the room, and Lewis gathered up the sheets of paper and took them to the window and began to read this:

I do not think that I can last much longer. We shared out the last drops of water a long time ago. I do not know how many days ago. We fall asleep and dream and walk about the house in our dreams, and I am often not sure whether I am awake or still dreaming, and so the days and nights are confused in my mind. I awoke not long ago, at least I suppose I awoke, and found I was lying in the passage.

There seems no hope for any of us. We are in the dream of death.

Here the manuscript became unintelligible for half a dozen lines. There was a fresh start, as it were, and the writer began again, in ordinary letter-form:

DEAR LEWIS:

I hope you will excuse all this confusion and wandering. I intended to begin a proper letter to you, and now I find all that stuff that you have been reading, if this ever gets into your hands. I have not the energy even to tear it up. If you read it you will know to what a sad pass I had come when it was written.

I have said of what I am writing, "if this ever gets into your hands," and I am not at all sure that it ever will. If what is happening here is happening everywhere else, then, I suppose, the world is coming to an end. I cannot understand it; even now I can hardly believe it.

And then there's another thing that bothers me. Now and then I wonder whether we are not all mad together in this house. Despite what I see and know, or, perhaps, I should say, because what I see and know is so impossible, I wonder whether we are not all suffering from a delusion. Perhaps we are our own jailers, and we are really free to go out and live. Perhaps what we think we see is not there at all. I wonder now and then whether we are all like this in Treff Loyne; yet in my heart I feel sure that it is not so.

Still, I do not want to leave a madman's letter behind me, and so I will not tell you the full story of what I have seen or believe I have seen. If I am a sane man, you will be able to fill in the blanks for yourself from your own knowledge. If I am mad, burn the letter and say nothing about it.

I think that it was on a Tuesday that we first noticed that there was something queer about. I came home about five or six o'clock and found the family at Treff Loyne laughing at old Tiger, the sheep-dog. He was making short runs from the farm-yard to the door of the house, barking, with quick, short yelps. Mrs. Griffith and Miss Griffith were standing by the porch, and the dog would go to them, look into their faces, and then run up the farm-yard to the gate, and then look back with that eager, yelping bark, as if he were waiting for the women to follow him. Then, again and again he ran up to them and tugged at their skirts, as if he would pull them by main force away from the house.

The dog barked and yelped and whined and scratched at the door all through the evening. They let him in once, but he seemed to have become quite frantic. He ran up to one member of the family after another; his eyes were bloodshot, and his mouth was foaming, and he tore at their clothes till they drove him out again into the darkness. Then he broke into a long, lamentable howl of anguish, and we heard no more of him.

It was soon after dawn when I finally roused myself. The people in the house were talking to each other in high voices, arguing about something that I did not understand.

"It is those damned Gipsies, I tell you," said old Griffith.

"What would they do a thing like that for?" asked Mrs. Griffith. "If it was stealing, now—"

They seemed puzzled and angry, so far as I could make out, but not at all frightened. I got up and began to dress. I don't think I looked out of the window. The glass on my dressing-table is high and broad, and the window is small; one would have to poke one's head round the glass to see anything.

The voices were still arguing down-stairs. I heard the old man say, "Well, here's for a beginning, anyhow," and then the door slammed.

A minute later the old man shouted, I think, to his son. Then there was a great noise which I will not describe more particularly, and a dreadful screaming and crying inside the house and a sound of rushing feet. They all cried out at once to each other. I heard the daughter crying: "It is no good, Mother; he is dead. Indeed they have killed him," and Mrs. Griffith screaming to the girl to let her go. And then one of them rushed out of the kitchen and shot the great bolts of oak across the door just as something beat against it with a thundering crash.

I ran down-stairs. I found them all in wild confusion, in an agony of grief and horror and amazement. They were like people who had seen something so awful that they had gone mad.

I went to the window looking out on the farm-yard. I won't tell you all that I saw, but I saw poor old Griffith lying by the pond, with the blood pouring out of his side.

I wanted to go out to him and bring him in. But they told me that he must be stone-dead, and such things also that it was quite plain that any one who went out of the house would not live more than a moment. We could not believe it even as we gazed at the body of the dead man; but it was there. I used to wonder sometimes what one would feel like if one saw an apple drop from the tree and shoot up into the air and disappear. I think I know now how one would feel.

Even then we couldn't believe that it would last. We were not seriously afraid for ourselves. We spoke of getting out in an hour or two, before dinner, anyhow. It couldn't last, because it was impossible. Indeed, at twelve o'clock young Griffith said he would go down to the well by the back way and draw another pail of water. I went to the door and stood by it. He had not gone a dozen yards before they were on him. He ran for his life, and we had all we could do to bar the door in time. And then I began to get frightened.

But day followed day, and it was still there. I went to Treff Loyne because it was buried in the narrow valley under the ash-trees, far away from any track. There was not so much as a footpath that was near it; no one ever came that way.

And now this thought came back without delight, with terror. Griffith thought that a shout might be heard on a still night up away on the Allt, "if a man was listening for it," he added doubtfully. My voice was clearer and stronger than his, and on the second night I said I would go up to my bedroom and call for help through the open window. I waited till it was all dark and still, and looked out through the window before opening it. And then I saw over the ridge of the long barn across the yard what looked like a tree, though I knew there was no tree there. It was a dark mass against the sky, with widespread boughs, a tree of thick, dense growth. I wondered what this could be, and I threw open the window not only because I was going to call for help, but because I wanted to see more clearly what the dark growth over the barn really was.

I saw in the depth of it points of fire, and colours in light, all glowing and moving, and the air trembled. I stared out into the night, and the dark tree lifted over the roof of the barn, rose up in the air, and floated toward me. I did not move till it was close to the house; and then I saw what it was, and banged the window down only just in time. I had to fight, and I saw the tree that was like a burning cloud rise up in the night and settle over the barn.

Another day went by, and at dusk I looked out, but the eyes of fire were watching me. I dared not open the window. And then I thought of another plan. There was the great old fireplace, with the round Flemish chimney going high above the house. If I stood beneath it and shouted, I thought perhaps the sound might be carried better than if I called out of the window; for all I knew the round chimney might act as a sort of megaphone. Night after night, then, I stood on the hearth and called for help from nine o'clock to eleven.

But we had drunk up the beer, and we would let ourselves have water only by little drops, and on the fourth night my throat was dry, and I began to feel strange and weak; I knew that all the voice I had in my lungs would hardly reach the length of the field by the farm.

It was then we began to dream of wells and fountains, and water coming very cold, in little drops, out of rocky places in the middle of a cool wood. We had given up all meals; now and then one would cut a lump from the sides of bacon on the kitchen wall and chew a bit of it, but the saltness was like fire.

And then we began to dream, as I say. And one day I dreamed that there was a bubbling well of cold, clear water in the cellar, and I had just hollowed my hand to drink it when I woke. I went into the kitchen and told young Griffith. I said I was sure there was water there. He shook his head, but he took up the great kitchen poker and we went down to the old cellar. I showed him the stone by the pillar, and he raised it up. But there was no well. Later I came upon young Griffith one evening evidently trying to make a subterranean passage under one of the walls of the house. I knew he was mad, as he knew I was mad when he saw me digging for a well in the cellar; but neither said anything to the other.

Now we are past all this. We are too weak. We dream when we are awake and when we dream we think we wake. Night and day come and go, and we mistake one for another.

Only a little while ago I heard a voice which sounded as if it were at my very ears, but rang and echoed and resounded as if it were rolling and reverberated from the vault of some cathedral, chanting in terrible modulations. I heard the words quite clearly, "Incipit liber iræ Domini Dei nostri" ("Here beginneth The Book of the Wrath of the Lord our God").

And then the voice sang the word *Aleph*, prolonging it, it seemed through ages, and a light was extinguished as it began the chapter:

"In that day, saith the Lord, there shall be a cloud over the land, and in the cloud a burning and a shape of fire, and out of the cloud shall issue forth my messengers; they shall run all together, they shall not turn aside; this shall be a day of exceeding bitterness, without salvation. And on every high hill, saith the Lord of Hosts, I will set my sentinels, and my armies shall encamp in the place of every valley; in the house that is amongst rushes I will execute judgment, and in vain shall they fly for refuge to the munitions of the rocks. In the groves of the woods, in the places where the leaves are as a tent above them, they shall find the sword of the slayer; and they that put their trust in walled cities shall be confounded. Woe unto the armed man, woe unto him that taketh pleasure in the strength of his artillery, for a little thing shall smite him, and by one that hath no might shall he be brought down into the dust. That which is low shall be set on high; I will make the lamb and the young sheep to be as the lion from the swellings of Jordan; they shall not spare, saith the Lord, and the doves shall be as eagles on the hill Engedi; none shall be found that may abide the onset of their battle."

Here the manuscript lapsed again and finally into utter, lamentable confusion of thought.

Dr. Lewis maintained that we should never begin to understand the real significance of life until we began to study just those aspects of it which we now dismiss and overlook as utterly inexplicable and therefore unimportant.

We were discussing a few months ago the awful shadow of the terror which at length had passed away from the land. I had formed my opinion, partly from observation, partly from certain facts which had been communicated to me, and the passwords having been exchanged, I found that Lewis had come by very different ways to the same end.

"And yet," he said, "it is not a true end, or, rather, it is like all the ends of human inquiry—it leads one to a great mystery. We must confess that what has happened might have happened at any time in the history of the world. It did not happen till a year ago, as a matter of fact, and therefore we made up our minds that it never could happen; or, one would better say, it was outside the range even of imagination. But this is our way. Most people are quite sure that the Black Death—otherwise the Plague—will never invade Europe again. They have made up their complacent minds that it was due to dirt and bad drainage. As a matter of fact the Plague had nothing to do with dirt or with drains, and there is nothing to prevent its ravaging England tomorrow. But if you tell people so, they won't believe you."

I agreed with all this. I added that sometimes the world was incapable of seeing, much less believing, that which was before its own eyes.

"Look," I said, "at any eighteenth-century print of a Gothic cathedral. You will find that the trained artistic eye even could not behold in any true sense the building that was before it. I have seen an old print of Peterborough Cathedral that looks as if the artist had drawn it from a clumsy model, constructed of bent wire and children's bricks."

"Exactly; because Gothic was outside the esthetic theory, and therefore vision, of the time. You can't believe what you don't see; rather, you can't see what you don't believe.

"You must not suppose that my experiences of that afternoon at Treff Loyne had afforded me the slightest illumination. Indeed, if it had not been that I had seen poor old Griffith's body lying pierced in his own farm-yard, I think I should have been inclined to accept one of Secretan's hints, and to believe that the whole family had fallen a victim to a collective delusion or hallucination, and had shut themselves up and died of thirst through sheer madness. I think there have been such cases. But I had seen the body of the murdered man and the wound that had killed him.

"Did the manuscript left by Secretan give me no hint? Well, it seemed to me to make confusion worse confounded. You see, Secretan, in writing that extraordinary document, almost insisted on the fact that he was not in his proper senses; that for days he had been part asleep, part awake, part delirious. How was one to judge his statement, to separate delirium from fact? In one thing he stood confirmed; you remember he speaks of calling for help up the old chimney of Treff Loyne; that did seem to fit in with the tales of a hollow, moaning cry that had been heard upon the Allt. So far one could take him as a recorder of actual experiences. And I looked in the old cellars of the farm and found a frantic sort of rabbit-hole dug by one of the pillars; again he was confirmed. But what was one to make of that story of the chanting voice and the letters of the Hebrew alphabet and the chapter out of some unknown minor prophet? When one has the key it is easy enough to sort out the facts or the hints of facts from the delusions; but I hadn't the key on that September evening. I was forgetting the 'tree' with lights and fires in it; that, I think, impressed me more than anything with the feeling that Secretan's story was in the main a true story. I had seen a like appearance down there in my own garden; but what was it?

"Now, I was saying that, paradoxically, it is only by the inexplicable things that life can be explained. We are apt to say, you know, 'a very odd coincidence,' and pass the matter by, as if there were no more to be said or as if that were the end of it. Well, I believe that the one real path lies through the blind alleys."

"How do you mean?"

"Well, this is an instance of what I mean. I was talking with Merritt, my brother-in-law, about the strange things he had seen in a way that I thought all nonsense, and I was wondering how I was going to shut him up when a big moth flew into the room through that window, fluttered about, and succeeded in burning itself alive in the lamp. That gave me my cue. I asked Merritt if he knew why moths made for lamps or something of the kind; I thought it would be a hint to him that I was sick of his half-baked theories. So it was; he looked sulky and held his tongue.

"But a few minutes later I was called out by a man who had found his little boy dead in a field near his cottage about an hour before. The child was so still, they said, that a great moth had settled on his forehead and fluttered away only when they lifted up the body. It was absolutely illogical; but it was this odd 'coincidence' of the moth in my lamp and the moth on the dead boy's forehead that first set me on the track. I can't say that it guided me in any real sense; it was more like a great flare of red paint on a wall.

"But, as you will remember, from having read my notes on the matter, I was called in about ten days later to see a man named Cradock who had been found in a field near his farm quite dead. This also was at night. His wife found him, and there were some very queer things in her story. She said that the hedge of the field looked as if it were changed; she began to be afraid that she had lost her way and got into the wrong field.

"Then came that extraordinary business of Treff Loyne. I took it all home, and sat down for the evening before it. It appalled me not only by its horror, but here again by the discrepancy between its terms.

"It was, I believe, a sudden leap of the mind that liberated me from the tangle. It was quite beyond logic. I went back to that evening when Merritt was boring me, to the moth in the candle, and to the moth on the forehead of poor Johnnie Roberts. There was no sense in it; but I suddenly determined that the child and Joseph Cradock the farmer, and that unnamed Stratfordshire man, all found at night, all asphyxiated, had been choked by vast swarms of moths. I don't pretend even now that this is demonstrated, but I'm sure it's true.

"Now suppose you encounter a swarm of these creatures in the dark. Suppose the smaller ones fly up your nostrils. You will gasp for breath and open your mouth. Then, suppose some hundreds of them fly into your mouth, into your gullet, into your windpipe, what will happen to you? You will be dead in a very short time, choked, asphyxiated."

"But the moths would be dead, too. They would be found in the bodies."

"The moths? Do you know that it is extremely difficult to kill a moth with cyanide of potassium? Take a frog, kill it, open its stomach. There you will find its dinner of moths and small beetles, and the 'dinner' will shake itself and walk off cheerily, to resume an entirely active existence. No; that is no difficulty.

"Well, now I came to this. I was shutting out all the other cases. I was confining myself to those that came under the one formula.

"Then the next step. Of course we know nothing really about moths; rather, we know nothing of moth reality. For all I know there may be hundreds of books which treat of moths and nothing but moths. But these are scientific books, and science deals only with surfaces. It has nothing to do with realities. To take a very minor matter: we don't even know why the moth desires the flame. But we do know what the moth does not do; it does not gather itself into swarms with the object of destroying human life. But here, by the hypothesis, were cases in which the moth had done this very thing; the moth race had entered, it seemed, into a malignant conspiracy against the human race. It was quite impossible, no doubt,—that is to say, it had never happened before,—but I could see no escape from this conclusion.

"These insects, then, were definitely hostile to man; and then I stopped, for I could not see the next step, obvious though it seems to me now. If the moths were infected with hatred of men, and possessed the design and the power of combining against him, why not suppose this hatred, this design, this power shared by other non-human creatures?

"The secret of the Terror might be condensed into a sentence: the animals had revolted against men.

"Now, the puzzle became easy enough; one had only to classify. Take the cases of the people who met their deaths by falling over cliffs or over the edge of quarries. We think of sheep as timid creatures, who always run away. But suppose sheep that don't run away; and, after all, in reason why should they run away? Quarry or no quarry, cliff or no cliff, what would happen to you if a hundred sheep ran after you instead of running from you? There would be no help for it; they would have you down and beat you to death or stifle you. Then suppose man, woman, or child near a cliff's edge or a quarry-side, and a sudden rush of sheep. Clearly there is no help; there is nothing for it but to go over. There can be no doubt that that is what happened in all these cases.

"And again. You know the country and you know how a herd of cattle will sometimes pursue people through the fields in a solemn, stolid sort of way. They behave as if they wanted to close in on you. Townspeople sometimes get frightened and scream and run; you or I would take no notice, or, at the utmost, would wave our sticks at the herd, which would stop dead or lumber off. But suppose they don't lumber off? It was a quicker death for poor Griffith of Treff Loyne: one of his own beasts gored him to death with one sharp thrust of its horn into his heart. And from that morning those within the house were closely besieged by their own cattle and horses and sheep, and when those unhappy people within opened a window to call for help or to catch a few drops of rain-water to relieve their burning thirst, the cloud waited for them with its myriad eyes of fire. Can you wonder that Secretan's statement reads in places like mania? You perceive the horrible position of those people in Treff Loyne; not only did they see death advancing on them, but advancing with incredible steps, as if one were to die not only in nightmare, but by nightmare. But no one in his wildest, most fiery dreams had ever imagined such a fate. I am not astonished that Secretan at one moment suspected the evidence of his own senses, at another surmised that the world's end had come."

"And how about the Williamses who were murdered on the Highway near here?"

"The horses were the murderers, the horses that afterward stampeded the camp below. By some means which is still obscure to me they lured that family into the road and beat their brains out; their shod hoofs were the instruments of execution. The munition-works? Their enemy was rats. I believe that it has been calculated that in 'greater London' the number of rats is about equal to the number of human beings; that is, there are about seven millions of them. The proportion would be about the same in all the great centres of population; and the rat, moreover, is on occasion migratory in its habits. You can understand now that story of the *Semiramis* beating about the mouth of the Thames, and at last cast away by Arcachon, her only crew dry heaps of bones. The rat is an expert boarder of ships. And so one can understand the tale told by the frightened man who took the path by the wood that led up from the new munition-works. He thought he heard a thousand men treading softly through the wood and chattering to one another in some horrible tongue; what he did hear was the marshalling of an army of rats, their array before the battle.

"And conceive the terror of such an attack. Even one rat in a fury is said to be an ugly customer to meet; conceive, then, the irruption of these terrible, swarming myriads, rushing upon the helpless, unprepared, astonished workers in the munition-shops."

There can be no doubt, I think, that Dr. Lewis was entirely justified in these extraordinary conclusions. As I say, I had arrived at pretty much the same end, by different ways; but this rather as to the general situation, while Lewis had made his own particular study of those circumstances of the Terror that were within his immediate purview, as a physician in large practice in the southern part of Meirion. Of some of the cases which he reviewed he had, no doubt, no immediate or first-hand knowledge; but he judged these instances by their similarity to the facts which had come under his personal notice. He spoke of the affairs of the quarry at Llanfihangel on the analogy of the people who were found dead at the bottom of the cliffs near Porth, and he was no doubt justified in doing so. He told me that, thinking the whole matter over, he was hardly more astonished by the Terror in itself than by the strange way in which he had arrived at his conclusions.

"You know," he said, "those certain evidences of animal malevolence which we knew of, the bees that stung the child to death, the trusted sheep-dogs turning savage, and so forth. Well, I got no light whatever from all this; it suggested nothing to me. You do not believe; therefore you cannot see.

"And then, when the truth at last appeared, it was through the whimsical 'coincidence,' as we call such signs, of the moth in my lamp and the moth on the dead child's forehead. This, I think, is very extraordinary."

"And there seems to have been one beast that remained faithful—the dog at Treff Loyne. That is strange."

"That remains a mystery."

It would not be wise, even now, to describe too closely the terrible scenes that were to be seen in the munition areas of the North and the Midlands during the black months of the Terror. Out of the factories issued at black midnight the shrouded dead in their coffins, and their very kinsfolk did not know how they had come by their deaths. All the towns were full of houses of mourning, were full of dark and terrible rumours as incredible as the incredible reality. There were things done and suffered that perhaps never will be brought to light, memories and secret traditions of these things will be whispered in families, delivered from father to son, growing wilder with the passage of the years, but never growing wilder than the truth.

It is enough to say that the cause of the Allies was for a while in deadly peril. The men at the front called in their extremity for guns and shells. No one told them what was happening in the places where these munitions were made.

But, after the first panic, measures were taken. The workers were armed with special weapons, guards were mounted, machine-guns were placed in position, bombs and liquid flame were ready against the obscene hordes of the enemy, and the "burning clouds" found a fire fiercer than their own. Many deaths occurred among the airmen; but they, too, were given special guns, arms that scattered shot broadcast, and so drove away the dark flights that threatened the airplanes.

And then, in the winter of 1915-16, the Terror ended suddenly as it had begun. Once more a sheep was a frightened beast that ran instinctively from a little child; the cattle were again solemn, stupid creatures, void of harm; the spirit and the convention of malignant design passed out of the hearts of all the animals. The chains that they had cast off for a while were thrown again about them.

And finally there comes the inevitable "Why?" Why did the beasts who had been humbly and patiently subject to man, or affrighted by his presence, suddenly know their strength and learn how to league together and declare bitter war against their ancient master?

It is a most difficult and obscure question. I give what explanation I have to give with very great diffidence, and an eminent disposition to be corrected if a clearer light can be found.

Some friends of mine, for whose judgment I have very great respect, are inclined to think that there was a certain contagion of hate. They hold that the fury of the whole world at war, the great passion of death that seems driving all humanity to destruction, infected at last these lower creatures, and in place of their native instinct of submission gave them rage and wrath and ravening.

This may be the explanation. I cannot say that it is not so, because I do not profess to understand the working of the universe. But I confess that the theory strikes me as fanciful. There may be a contagion of hate as there is a contagion of smallpox; I do not know, but I hardly believe it.

In my opinion, and it is only an opinion, the source of the great revolt of the beasts is to be sought in a much subtler region of inquiry. I believe that the subjects revolted because the king abdicated. Man has dominated the beasts throughout the ages, the spiritual has reigned over the rational through the peculiar quality and grace of spirituality that men possess, that makes a man to be that which he is. And when he maintained this power and grace, I think it is pretty clear that between him and the animals there was a certain treaty and alliance. There was supremacy on the one hand and submission on the other; but at the same time there was between the two that cordiality which exists between lords and subjects in a well-organized state. I know a socialist who maintains that Chaucer's "Canterbury Tales" give a picture of true democracy. I do not know about that, but I see that knight and miller were able to get on quite pleasantly together, just because the knight knew that he was a knight and the miller knew that he was a miller. If the knight had had conscientious objections to his knightly grade, while the miller saw no reason why he should not be a knight, I am sure that their intercourse would have been difficult, unpleasant, and perhaps murderous.

So with man. I believe in the strength and truth of tradition. A learned man said to me a few weeks ago: "When I have to choose between the evidence of tradition and the evidence of a document, I always believe the evidence of tradition. Documents may be falsified and often are falsified; tradition is never falsified." This is true; and therefore, I think, one may put trust in the vast body of folklore which asserts that there was once a worthy and friendly alliance between man and the beasts. Our popular tale of Dick Whittington and his cat no doubt represents the adaptation of a very ancient legend to a comparatively modern personage, but we may go back into the ages and find the popular tradition asserting that not only are the animals the subjects, but also the friends of man.

All that was in virtue of that singular spiritual element in man which the rational animals do not possess. Spiritual does not mean respectable, it does not even mean moral, it does not mean "good" in the ordinary acceptation of the word. It signifies the royal prerogative of man, differentiating him from the beasts.

For long ages he has been putting off this royal robe, he has been wiping the balm of consecration from his own breast. He has declared again and again that he is not spiritual, but rational; that is, the equal of the beasts over whom he was once sovereign. He has vowed that he is not Orpheus, but Caliban.

But the beasts also have within them something which corresponds to the spiritual quality in men; we are content to call it instinct. They perceived that the throne was vacant; not even friendship was possible between them and the self-deposed monarch. If he was not king, he was a sham, an impostor, a thing to be destroyed.

Hence, I think, the Terror. They have risen once; they may rise again.

In the year 1918

27 Jan.   The Finnish Civil War between White and Red Finland begins with the Battle of Kämärä.

6 Feb.   The Representation of the People Act gives the vote to most women over 30 in Britain.

3 March   Soviet Russia and the Central Powers sign the Treaty of Brest-Litovsk, ending Russian Involvement in World War I.

11 March   Over 500 cases of Spanish flu documented at Fort Riley in Kansas, USA.

21 March   Beginning of the German Spring Offensive along the Western Front.

7 April   The Fourth Battle of Ypres (The Battle of the Lys) begins in Belgium.

21 April   German fighter pilot ace Baron Manfred von Richthofen ("The Red Baron") is shot down and killed over Vaux-sur-Somme in France.

17 July   Former Tsar Nicholas II, his family, and his retainers are murdered by the Bolsheviks.

3 Aug.   British troops land in Vladivostok, Russia, as part of the Siberian Intervention launched by the Allies to support White Russian forces and the Czechoslovak Legion against Soviet Russia.

8 Aug.   Beginning of the Battle of Amiens in France, fought between the Allies and Germany.

19 Sept.   Start of the Battle of Megiddo in Palestine.

3 Nov.   The Austro-Hungarian Empire enters an armistice to end the war on the Italian front.

9 Nov.   Kaiser Wilhelm II of Germany abdicates and the Weimar Republic is proclaimed.

11 Nov.   Germany signs an armistice agreement with the Allies, ending World War I.

− 1918 −

The Middle Bedroom

Henry de Vere Stacpoole

Are all living creatures represented in the human race, so that we find shark men—or, at least, men with the instincts of sharks—sloth men, cat men, tiger men, and so on? Le Brun started the idea, I believe, and I take it up as bearing on the case of Sir Michael Carey, of Carey House, near Innis Town, on the west coast of Ireland.

I would ask another question before starting on my story: If a man were to give way to his natural instincts and retire from the world would he develop, or, rather, degenerate, along the line of his main instinct? Who can say? I only know that Sir Michael, the builder of the house that took his name, was known a hundred years ago amongst the illiterate peasantry as "the spider." That, so dubbed on account of his mentality and general make-up, he lived alone in his house like a spider in a gloomy corner. That, according to legend, the devil came and took him one dark night, leaving neither rag nor bone of him and that his ghost was reputed to haunt Carey House and the country round, ever after.

The next of kin, Mr. Massy Pope, tried to live in the house. He left suddenly on account of the "loneliness" of the situation and succeeded in letting the place, with the shooting and fishing rights, to a hard-headed Englishman named Doubleday.

Doubleday didn't believe in ghosts nor care about them.

Snipe was his game—and cock. He was a two-bottle man—it was in 1863—and if he had met with a ghost any time after ten o'clock he would scarcely have seen it, or seeing it, would not have cared. But his servants were the trouble. They left one day in a body, being soft-headed folk and unfortified and having a very good reason of their own. Then some years elapsed and the story of the next let, as told to me by Micky Feelan one day, out shooting, was as follows:

"When Mr. Doubleday had gone, sor, the house laid empty, sp'ilin' the country for miles round, not a man would go into the groun's to trap a rabbit nor a woman enter its doors to lift a window, and Mr. Pope squanderin' his money to advertise it. That's the man he was, he wouldn't be bet by it, rowlin' in riches what did it matter to him whether it lay let or empty, not a brass farthing, but he wouldn't be bet by it, it was like a horse that wouldn't rise at a ditch, and he'd canther it back and try it again and lather it over the head, squanderin' his money on the advertisin' till all of a sudden he got a rise out of a family be name of Leftwidge.

"Dublin people they were, with a grocer's shop in old Fishamble Street. There was a dozen of them, mostly childer and one red-headed strip of a girl to do the cookin'. Twenty pound a year was the rent, I've heard tell, and they lived mostly be trappin' rabbits, the boys doin' a bit of fishin' and the groceries comin' from the shop where the ould father stuck at work in his shirt sleeves while the rest of the lot was airin' themselves in the counthry.

"Be jabers, they were a crowd. Ghosts! Little they cared about ghosts shamblin' about widout shoes or stockin's and the boys wid their sticks and catapaults killin' hens be the sly and maltreatin' the country boys like Red Injuns, the shame of the county.

"Norah Driscol was the name of the red-headed slip and

many a time me mother has seen her wid her apron over her head rockin' and cryin' wid the treatment of them boys and the botheration of the rest of them, for there was a matter of a dozen or more, rangin' like the pipes of an organ from Micky the eldest son six fut and as thin as a gas pipe, to Pat the youngest not the height of your knee.

"Well, sor, the ghost lay aisy at the sight of the lot of them and didn't let a word out of it for a full month. Then, one day, Norah Driscoll was goin' along the top flure passage whin the band begin to play. The bedrooms was mostly on that passage and the house agent had warned them against havin' anythin' to do with the middle-most bedroom, for, says he, there's rats there that can't be got rid of and that's the cause of all the trouble in the lettin' of the house, says he. It would be a hundred and twenty a year rent, only for them rats, says he, so they're worth a hundred a year to you if you just keep the door shut and don't bother about the noises they do be makin' at odd times—sometimes it's like as if they was sneezin' and blowin' their noses and sometimes it's like as if they was walkin' about with their brogues on and sometimes it's like as if they was cursin' and swearin'. Don't you mind them, he says, but keep sayin' over and over to yourself they're worth a hundred a year to me. That's what he tould Mrs. Leftwidge.

"Well, sor, Norah was moonin' along the passage, sent to fetch a duster or somethin' when she opened the dure of the middle bedroom be mistake. There was no furniture in it, not as much as a three-legged stool and the blind was down, but a shaft of sun struck through be the side of the blind and there in the middle of the flure was sittin' a little old man dressed as they was dressed a hundred years ago in an ould brown coat wid brass buttons and all and the face of him under his hat topped the sight of him, for Norah said it wasn't a face, but more like one of those masks the childer make out of a bit of paper with holes in it.

"The screech she let out of her as she banged the dure to, brought the family runnin' from downstairs, and the boys slammed open the door to get at the chap but there wasn't a speck of him.

" 'It's a rat she saw' says Mrs. Leftwidge. 'Downstairs wid the lot of you or I'll give you the linth of me slipper—and open that dure again if you dare.'

"Down they went, Norah bawlin' and the old woman pushin' her and nothin' more happened that day till the night. Half a dozen of the little ones slep' in the same room with their mother to save the light and be under control and gettin' on for twelve o'clock the old woman, snorin' wid her mouth wide, was woke up from her slape be one of the childer.

" 'Mummy,' says he, 'listen to the bagpipes.'

"She lifted herself on her elbow, but, faith, she could have heard it with her head under the clothes, for the dhrone of the pipes filled the house comin' from the middle bedroom.

"Next minit the whole lither of them was in the passage, the old woman with a gutherin' candle in her hand, and as they stood there keepin' time with their teeth to the tune of the pipes, the noise of it suddenly let off and the handle of the middle bedroom dure began to turn.

"They didn't wait to see what was comin' out; no, your honour, you may bet your life they didn't, they was half of them under their beds the linth of that night and next mornin' they began to pack to go back to Dublin, gettin' their old traps together and strippin' the garden to take back wid them in hampers. Micky, the second boy, was sent runnin' to hire two cars to take them to the station, for the railway in those days had just come to Drumboyne, twelve miles away, and whilst he was gone they tore up the potatoes and cut the cabbages and faith they'd have taken the flurin' away if they'd had manes to shift it.

"Well, there they were strapped and ready to go when Mrs. Leftwidge, sittin' in her bonnet on the boxes and atin' a sand-widge, suddenly stops her chewin' and looks about her like a hen countin' her chickens:

" 'Where's Pat?' says she.

"Pat was the youngest, as I've tould you, sor, a bit of a chap in petticoats, no size at all and always gettin' astray.

" 'I don't know,' says one of the boys, 'but faith, I hear him shoutin' somewhere upstairs.'

"Upstairs they all rushed led be the woman and they hadn't no sooner reached the top passage than they seen Pat bein' whisked through the open dure of the middle bedroom, dragged along be somebody's hand, and when they reached the dure, there was Pat bein' dragged up the chimney.

"It was one of them big ould chimneys a man could go up, and the heels of the child was disappearin' when Mrs. Left-widge lays hold of a fut and pulls, bawlin' murder Irish, till the thing in the chimney let go its holt and Pat comes into the grate, kickin' like a pup in the shtrangles and liftin' the roof off with the hullabaloo of him.

"She tuck him be one fut like a turkey and down she runs with him and into the garden and there when they'd soothed him he gives his story, how he'd been playin in the passage when a little ould man, the funniest ould man he'd ever seen pokes his head out of the bedroom dure. Pat, poor divil, bein' sated at his play couldn't get his legs under him wid the fright; he could only sit and shout whilst the head of the little ould man pops in and out of the dureway like the head of a tortoise from its shell.

"Then out he comes the whole of him and grabs the child be the hand and whisks him off into the bedroom and goes up the chimney heels first, haulin' Pat afther him. Goes up like a spider.

"Well, they was sittin' about on the boxes they'd hauled out of the house waitin' for the cars and tryin' to squeeze more of the news out of Pat, when up comes the cars wid Sergeant Rafferty and Constable O'Halloran on wan of them, to see they weren't takin' the house away wid them—they'd got that bad name in the county.

"And when the sergeant heard the story, up he went to the bedroom and down he comes again.

" 'Here,' says he to O'Halloran, 'take this lot off to the train and go to the barracks and fetch me two carbines wid buck-shot ca'tridges—the same ould Forster used to shoot the boys with, bad luck to him—and look slippy,' says he, 'for I'm a brave man, but I don't want to be no longer here be myself than's needful.'

"Off the cars went wid the family packed like flies on them an' in a matter of a couple of hours back comes the constable wid the guns. Up they go to the bedroom.

" 'Stick your head up the chimney,' says the sergeant.

" 'I'll be — if do,' says the other.

" 'Well, then, shut it,' says the sergeant, 'and keep still.'

"They listened but they didn't hear nothing at all. Then the sergeant begins talkin' in a loud voice, winkin' at the other.

" 'There's nothin' there,' says he, 'it was a ghost they saw and it's gettin' oneasy I am meself. Let's get off back to Drumboyne and have a glass and lave the ould house to look afther itself.'

" 'I'm wid you,' says the constable and downstairs they tramped, makin' as much noise wid their big boots as a rigiment of soldiers. Then in the hall they sits down and begins takin' off their boots.

" 'All the same,' says the constable as he pulled the laces, 'I'd be just as aisy in me mind if I was three miles off trampin' on the road to Drumboyne.'

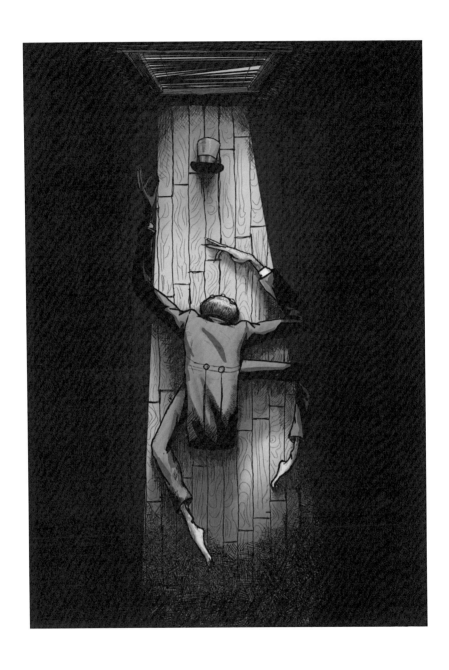

For that chap was a spider, sor, they said his face was the face of a spider, and his arms and legs no better.

" 'So would I,' says the sergeant, 'and it's there I'd be, only I'm thinkin' of promotion.'

" 'I'm thinkin' of ghosts,' says the constable wid the boot-lace in his hand.

" 'Go on unlacin' your boots,' says the other, 'and don't be a keyoward, this is no ghost. Ghosts can't pull childer up chimneys.'

" 'Faith, you seem to know a lot about them,' says the constable, 'but it's I that am thinkin' it's holy water and Father Mooney ought to be on this job instead of you and me and guns.'

" 'And how would you get holy water up the chimney?' axes the sergeant then.

" 'Wit a squirt,' replies him, 'and how else?'

" 'Squirt yourself out of them boots,' says the sergeant, 'or it's me ramrod I'll take to you, and now follow me,' he says, 'and walk soft.'

"Wid the loaded guns in their hands up they wint makin' no more sound than shaddas in a wall, and when they got to the room down they squats one on each side of the chimney.

"They hears nothin' for a while, but the tickin' of the sergeant's watch, and the sounds of their own hearts goin' lub-a-dub. Then comes a cough. It wasn't a right sort of cough, for, let alone that it was comin' down a chimney, it sounded to be the cough of a chap that had died for want of water and lain in a brick kiln afther.

"The constable said next day he'd have been up and off only the sound cut the legs from under him, the sergeant wasn't much better and there they sat sayin' their prayers and listenin' for more.

"They waited near an hour hearin nothin', and then all at once began a noise, a scratchin' and a scrabblin' like a cat comin' down a drain pipe.

" 'It's comin down,' shouts the constable.

" 'Begob it's not,' says the sergeant and wid that he shoves the muzzle of his gun up the flue and fires.

"He fired from fright to keep it up, so he said at the inquest, but, be jabers, he brought it down like a cock pheasant, tumblin' and clawin' and when they stretched it out on the flure it was a man right enough. A bit of an ould man as brown as a spider, and there he lay dead as a grouse wid the buckshot holes in him and not a drop of blood no more than if he'd been made of cardboard.

" 'Cover the face of him,' says the constable, for that was the sort of face he had, better than I can tell you, and havin' nothin' to cover it they turned him face down, and made off runnin' to Drumboyne for the residint magistrit.

"Well, sor, when they took that chimney down they found a room off it, all littered with bones and birds feathers and rats' tails. It wouldn't do to be tellin' you of that room, more than it had no winda to it and had been built on purpose be Sir Michael Carey when he put the house up. He'd took to live in it, for that was the way his heart was, and at long last he took to live nowhere else, and that was how the sergeant brought him down and he must have been a matter of a hundred and tin years of age, they reckoned.

"He had his bagpipes to cheer him and frighten away tinints and he'd be out be nights scavengin' for food—they say they found the bones of childer in the room, but may be that was a lie got be him tryin' to drag Pat Leftwidge up the flue— but faith I wouldn't put it beyond him. For that chap was a spider, sor, they said his face was the face of a spider, and his arms and legs no better.

"He'd begun in the shape of a man, maybe, but the spider in him got the bether of him. Look, there's all there's left of the house, sor, thim walls beyond the trees. They set a light to it to get shut of that room and if you knew the truth of it all you wouldn' blame them."

In the year 1919

2 Jan.	Soviet forces invade Ukraine.
6 Jan.	Former US President Theodore Roosevelt dies aged 60 at his home in Oyster Bay, New York.
18 Jan.	Opening of the Paris Peace Conference, attended by diplomats from 32 countries.
21 Jan.	Sinn Féin declares Irish independence and two Royal Irish Constabulary officers are shot by IRA volunteers, leading to the Anglo-Irish War.
14 Feb.	The first engagement of the Polish-Soviet War takes place at Bereza Kartuska.
2–6 March	The 1st Congress of the Communist International is held in Moscow.
23 March	Benito Mussolini founds the *Fasci Italiani di Combattimento* (predecessor of the National Fascist Party) in Milan, Italy.
10 April	Mexican Civil War: revolutionary Emiliano Zapata is ambushed and shot dead.
4 May	May Fourth Movement: protests in Beijing against transfer of Chinese territories to Japan.
6 May	American author L. Frank Baum dies aged 62 in Los Angeles, California.
19 May	Turkish War of Independence: future president Mustafa Kemal Atatürk arrives at Samsun.
21 June	Admiral Ludwig von Reuter scuttles the German fleet interned at Scapa Flow, Scotland to prevent its seizure by Britain.
28 June	The Treaty of Versailles is signed, formally ending World War I.
16 Oct.	Adolf Hitler presents his first speech to the German Workers' Party (Deutsche Arbeiterpartei).

— 1919 —

Unseen—Unfeared

Francis Stevens
(Gertrude Barrows Bennett)

I.

I had been dining with my ever-interesting friend, Mark Jenkins, at a little Italian restaurant near South Street. It was a chance meeting. Jenkins is too busy, usually, to make dinner engagements. Over our highly seasoned food and sour, thin, red wine, he spoke of little odd incidents and adventures of his profession. Nothing very vital or important, of course. Jenkins is not the sort of detective who first detects and then pours the egotistical and revealing details of achievement in the ears of every acquaintance, however appreciative.

But when I spoke of something I had seen in the morning papers, he laughed. "Poor old 'Doc' Holt! Fascinating old codger, to anyone who really knows him. I've had his friendship for years—since I was first on the city force and saved a young assistant of his from jail on a false charge. And they had to drag him into the poisoning of this young sport, Ralph Peeler!"

"Why are you so sure he couldn't have been implicated?" I asked.

But Jenkins only shook his head, with a quiet smile. "I have reasons for believing otherwise," was all I could get out of him on that score, "But," he added, "the only reason he was suspected at all is the superstitious dread of these ignorant people around him. Can't see why he lives in such a place. I know for a fact he doesn't have to. Doc's got money of his own. He's an amateur chemist and dabbler in different sorts of research work, and I suspect he's been guilty of 'showing off.' Result, they all swear he has the evil eye and holds forbidden communion with invisible powers. Smoke?"

Jenkins offered me one of his invariably good cigars, which I accepted, saying thoughtfully: "A man has no right to trifle with the superstitions of ignorant people. Sooner or later, it spells trouble."

"Did in his case. They swore up and down that he sold love charms openly and poisons secretly, and that, together with his living so near to—somebody else—got him temporarily suspected. But my tongue's running away with me, as usual!"

"As usual," I retorted impatiently, "you open up with all the frankness of a Chinese diplomat."

He beamed upon me engagingly and rose from the table, with a glance at his watch. "Sorry to leave you, Blaisdell, but I have to meet Jimmy Brennan in ten minutes."

He so clearly did not invite my further company that I remained seated for a little while after his departure; then took my own way homeward. Those streets always held for me a certain fascination, particularly at night. They are so unlike the rest of the city, so foreign in appearance, with their little shabby stores, always open until late evening, their unbelievably cheap goods, displayed as much outside the shops as in them, hung on the fronts and laid out on tables by the curb and in the street itself. Tonight, however, neither people nor stores in any sense appealed to me. The mixture of Italians, Jews and a few negroes,[1] mostly bareheaded, unkempt and

---

1   Text presented as originally published in *People's Favorite Magazine*; see Introduction (page VII).

generally unhygienic in appearance, struck me as merely revolting. They were all humans, and I, too, was human. Some way I did not like the idea.

Puzzled a trifle, for I am more inclined to sympathize with poverty than accuse it, I watched the faces that I passed. Never before had I observed how bestial, how brutal were the countenances of the dwellers in this region. I actually shuddered when an old-clothes man, a gray-bearded Hebrew, brushed me as he toiled past with his barrow.

There was a sense of evil in the air, a warning of things which it is wise for a clean man to shun and keep clear of. The impression became so strong that before I had walked two squares I began to feel physically ill. Then it occurred to me that the one glass of cheap Chianti I had drunk might have something to do with the feeling. Who knew how that stuff had been manufactured, or whether the juice of the grape entered at all into its ill-flavoured composition? Yet I doubted if that were the real cause of my discomfort.

By nature I am rather a sensitive, impressionable sort of chap. In some way tonight this neighbourhood, with its sordid sights and smells, had struck me wrong.

My sense of impending evil was merging into actual fear. This would never do. There is only one way to deal with an imaginative temperament like mine—conquer its vagaries. If I left South Street with this nameless dread upon me, I could never pass down it again without a recurrence of the feeling. I should simply have to stay here until I got the better of it— that was all.

I paused on a corner before a shabby but brightly lighted little drug store. Its gleaming windows and the luminous green of its conventional glass show jars made the brightest spot on the block. I realized that I was tired, but hardly wanted to go in there and rest. I knew what the company would be like at its shabby, sticky soda fountain. As I stood there, my eyes fell on a long white canvas sign across from me, and its black-and-red lettering caught my attention.

SEE THE GREAT UNSEEN!
COME IN! THIS MEANS YOU!
FREE TO ALL!

A museum of fakes, I thought, but also reflected that if it were a show of some kind I could sit down for a while, rest, and fight off this increasing obsession of nonexistent evil. That side of the street was almost deserted, and the place itself might well be nearly empty.

II.

I walked over, but with every step my sense of dread increased. Dread of I knew not what. Bodiless, inexplicable horror had me as in a net, whose strands, being intangible, without reason for existence, I could by no means throw off. It was not the people now. None of them were about me. There, in the open, lighted street, with no sight nor sound of terror to assail me, I was the shivering victim of such fear as I had never known was possible. Yet still I would not yield.

Setting my teeth, and fighting with myself as with some pet animal gone mad, I forced my steps to slowness and walked along the sidewalk, seeking entrance. Just here there were no shops, but several doors reached in each case by means of a few iron-railed stone steps. I chose the one in the middle beneath the sign. In that neighborhood there are museums, shops and other commercial enterprises conducted in many shabby old residences, such as were these. Behind the glazing of the door I had chosen I could see a dim, pinkish light, but on either side the windows were quite dark.

Trying the door, I found it unlocked. As I opened it a party of Italians passed on the pavement below and I looked back at them over my shoulder. They were gayly dressed, men, women and children, laughing and chattering to one another; probably on their way to some wedding or other festivity.

In passing, one of the men glanced up at me and involuntarily I shuddered back against the door. He was a young man, handsome after the swarthy manner of his race, but never in my life had I seen a face so expressive of pure, malicious cruelty, naked and unashamed. Our eyes met and his seemed to light up with a vile gleaming, as if all the wickedness of his nature had come to a focus in the look of concentrated hate he gave me.

They went by, but for some distance I could see him watching me, chin on shoulder, till he and his party were swallowed up in the crowd of marketers farther down the street.

Sick and trembling from that encounter, merely of eyes though it had been, I threw aside my partly smoked cigar and entered. Within there was a small vestibule, whose ancient tesselated floor was grimy with the passing of many feet. I could feel the grit of dirt under my shoes, and it rasped on my rawly quivering nerves. The inner door stood partly open, and going on I found myself in a bare, dirty hallway, and was greeted by the sour, musty, poverty-stricken smell common to dwellings of the very ill-to-do. Beyond there was a stairway, carpeted with ragged grass matting. A gas jet, turned low inside a very dusty pink globe, was the light I had seen from without.

Listening, the house seemed entirely silent. Surely, this was no place of public amusement of any kind whatever. More likely it was a rooming house, and I had, after all, mistaken the entrance.

To my intense relief, since coming inside, the worst agony of my unreasonable terror had passed away. If I could only get in some place where I could sit down and be quiet, probably

I should be rid of it for good. Determining to try another entrance, I was about to leave the bare hallway when one of several doors along the side of it suddenly opened and a man stepped out into the hall.

"Well?" he said, looking at me keenly, but with not the least show of surprise at my presence.

"I beg your pardon," I replied. "The door was unlocked and I came in here, thinking it was the entrance to the exhibit—what do they call it?—the 'Great Unseen.' The one that is mentioned on that long white sign. Can you tell me which door is the right one?"

"I can."

With that brief answer he stopped and stared at me again. He was a tall, lean man, somewhat stooped, but possessing considerable dignity of bearing. For that neighborhood, he appeared uncommonly well dressed, and his long, smooth-shaven face was noticeable because, while his complexion was dark and his eyes coal-black, above them the heavy brows and his hair were almost silvery-white. His age might have been anything over the threescore mark.

I grew tired of being stared at. "If you can and—won't, then never mind," I observed a trifle irritably, and turned to go. But his sharp exclamation halted me.

"No!" he said. "No—no! Forgive me for pausing—it was not hesitation, I assure you. To think that one—one, even, has come! All day they pass my sign up there—pass and fear to enter. But you are different. *You* are not of these timorous, ignorant foreign peasants. You ask me to tell you the right door? Here it is! Here!"

And he struck the panel of the door, which he had closed behind him, so that the sharp yet hollow sound of it echoed up through the silent house.

Now it may be thought that after all my senseless terror in the open street, so strange a welcome from so odd a showman would have brought the feeling back, full force. But there is an emotion stronger, to a certain point, than fear. This queer old fellow aroused my curiosity. What kind of museum could it be that he accused the passing public of fearing to enter? Nothing really terrible, surely, or it would have been closed by the police. And normally I am not an unduly timorous person. "So it's in there, is it?" I asked, coming toward him. "And I'm to be sole audience? Come, that will be an interesting experience." I was half laughing now.

"The most interesting in the world," said the old man, with a solemnity which rebuked my lightness.

With that he opened the door, passed inward and closed it again—in my very face. I stood staring at it blankly. The panels, I remember, had been originally painted white, but now the paint was flaked and blistered, gray with dirt and dirty finger marks. Suddenly it occurred to me that I had no wish to enter there. Whatever was behind it could be scarcely worth seeing, or he would not choose such a place for its exhibition. With the old man's vanishing my curiosity had cooled, but just as I again turned to leave, the door opened and this singular showman stuck his white-eyebrowed face through the aperture. He was frowning impatiently. "Come in—come in!" he snapped, and promptly withdrawing his head, once more closed the door.

"He has something there he doesn't want should get out," was the very natural conclusion which I drew. "Well, since it can hardly be anything dangerous, and he's so anxious I should see it—here goes!"

With that I turned the soiled white porcelain handle, and entered.

The room I came into was neither very large nor very brightly lighted. In no way did it resemble a museum or lecture room. On the contrary, it seemed to have been fitted up as a quite well-appointed laboratory. The floor was linoleum-covered, there were glass cases along the walls whose shelves were filled with bottles, specimen jars, graduates, and the like. A large table in one corner bore what looked like some odd sort of camera, and a larger one in the middle of the room was fitted with a long rack filled with bottles and test tubes, and was besides littered with papers, glass slides, and various paraphernalia which my ignorance failed to identify. There were several cases of books, a few plain wooden chairs, and in the corner a large iron sink with running water.

My host of the white hair and black eyes was awaiting me, standing near the larger table. He indicated one of the wooden chairs with a thin forefinger that shook a little, either from age or eagerness. "Sit down—sit down! Have no fear but that you will be interested, my friend. Have no fear at all—of anything!"

As he said it he fixed his dark eyes upon me and stared harder than ever. But the effect of his words was the opposite of their meaning. I did sit down, because my knees gave under me, but if in the outer hall I had lost my terror, it now returned twofold upon me. Out there the light had been faint, dingily roseate, indefinite. By it I had not perceived how this old man's face was a mask of living malice—of cruelty, hate and a certain masterful contempt. Now I knew the meaning of my fear, whose warning I would not heed. Now I knew that I had walked into the very trap from which my abnormal sensitiveness had striven in vain to save me.

III.

Again I struggled within me, bit at my lip till I tasted blood, and presently the blind paroxysm passed. It must have been longer in going than I thought, and the old man must have all that time been speaking, for when I could once more control my attention, hear and see him, he had taken up a position near the sink, about ten feet away, and was addressing me with a sort of "platform" manner, as if I had been the large audience whose absence he had deplored.

"And so," he was saying, "I was forced to make these plates very carefully, to truly represent the characteristic hues of each separate organism. Now, in color work of every kind the film is necessarily extremely sensitive. Doubtless you are familiar in a general way with the exquisite transparencies produced by color photography of the single-plate type."

He paused, and trying to act like a normal human being, I observed: "I saw some nice landscapes done in that way—last week at an illustrated lecture in Franklin Hall."

He scowled, and made an impatient gesture at me with his hand. "I can proceed better without interruptions," he said. "My pause was purely oratorical."

I meekly subsided, and he went on in his original loud, clear voice. He would have made an excellent lecturer before a much larger audience—if only his voice could have lost that eerie, ringing note. Thinking of that I must have missed some more, and when I caught it again he was saying:

"As I have indicated, the original plate is the final picture. Now, many of these organisms are extremely hard to photograph, and microphotography in color is particularly difficult. In consequence, to spoil a plate tries the patience of the photographer. They are so sensitive that the ordinary dark-room ruby lamp would instantly ruin them, and they must therefore be developed either in darkness or by a special light produced by interposing thin sheets of tissue of a particular shade of green and of yellow between lamp and plate, and even that will often cause ruinous fog. Now I, finding it hard to handle them so, made numerous experiments with a view of discovering some glass or fabric of a color which should add to the safety of the green, without robbing it of all efficiency. All proved equally useless, but intermittently I persevered—until last week."

His voice dropped to an almost confidential tone, and he leaned slightly toward me. I was cold from my neck to my feet, though my head was burning, but I tried to force an appreciative smile.

"Last week," he continued impressively, "I had a prescription filled at the corner drug store. The bottle was sent home to me wrapped in a piece of what I at first took to be whitish, slightly opalescent paper. Later I decided that it was some kind of membrane. When I questioned the druggist, seeking its source, he said it was a sheet of 'paper' that was around a bundle of herbs from South America. That he had no more, and doubted if I could trace it. He had wrapped my bottle so, because he was in haste and the sheet was handy.

"I can hardly tell you what first inspired me to try that membrane in my photographic work. It was merely dull white with a faint hint of opalescence, except when held against the light. Then it became quite translucent and quite brightly prismatic. For some reason it occurred to me that this refractive effect might help in breaking up the actinic rays—the rays which affect the sensitive emulsion. So that night I inserted it behind the sheets of green and yellow tissue, next the lamp, prepared my trays and chemicals, laid my plate holders to hand, turned off the white light and—turned on the green!"

There was nothing in his words to inspire fear. It was a wearisomely detailed account of his struggles with photography. Yet, as he again paused impressively, I wished that he might never speak again. I was desperately, contemptibly in dread of the thing he might say next.

Suddenly he drew himself erect, the stoop went out of his shoulders, he threw back his head and laughed. It was a hollow sound, as if he laughed into a trumpet. "I won't tell you what I saw! Why should I? Your own eyes shall bear witness. But this much I'll say, so that you may better understand—later. When our poor, faultily sensitive vision can perceive a thing, we say that it is visible. When the nerves of touch can feel it, we say that it is tangible. Yet I tell you there are beings intangible to our physical sense, yet whose presence is felt by the spirit, and invisible to our eyes merely because those organs are not attuned to the light as reflected from their bodies. But light passed through the screen which we are about to use has a wavelength novel to the scientific world, and by it you shall see with the eyes of the flesh that which has been invisible since life began. Have no fear!"

He stopped to laugh again, and his mirth was yellow-toothed—menacing.

"*Have no fear!*" he reiterated, and with that stretched his hand toward the wall, there came a click and we were in black, impenetrable darkness. I wanted to spring up, to seek the door by which I had entered and rush out of it, but the paralysis of unreasoning terror held me fast.

I could hear him moving about in the darkness, and a moment later a faint green glimmer sprang up in the room. Its source was over the large sink, where I suppose he developed his precious "color plates."

Every instant, as my eyes became accustomed to the dimness, I could see more clearly. Green light is peculiar. It may be far fainter than red, and at the same time far more illuminating. The old man was standing beneath it, and his face by that ghastly radiance had the exact look of a dead man's. Beside this, however, I could observe nothing appalling.

"That," continued the man, "is the simple developing light of which I have spoken—now watch, for what you are about to behold no mortal man but myself has ever seen before."

For a moment he fussed with the green lamp over the sink. It was so constructed that all the direct rays struck downward. He opened a flap at the side, for a moment there was a streak of comforting white luminance from within, then he inserted something, slid it slowly in—and closed the flap.

The thing he put in—that South American "membrane" it must have been—instead of decreasing the light increased it—amazingly. The hue was changed from green to greenish-gray, and the whole room sprang into view, a livid, ghastly chamber, filled with—overcrawled by—what?

My eyes fixed themselves, fascinated, on something that moved by the old man's feet. It writhed there on the floor like a huge, repulsive starfish, an immense, armed, legged thing, that twisted convulsively. It was smooth, as if made of rubber, was whitish-green in color; and presently raised its great round blob of a body on tottering tentacles, crept toward my host and writhed upward—yes, climbed up his legs, his body. And he stood there, erect, arms folded, and stared sternly down at the thing which climbed.

But the room—the whole room was alive with other creatures than that. Everywhere I looked they were—centipedish things, with yard-long bodies, detestable, furry spiders that lurked in shadows, and sausage-shaped translucent horrors that moved—and floated through the air. They dived here and there between me and the light, and I could see its brighter greenness through their greenish bodies.

Worse, though, far worse than these were the *things with human faces*. Mask-like, monstrous, huge gaping mouths and slitlike eyes—I find I cannot write of them. There was that about them which makes their memory even now intolerable.

The old man was speaking again, and every word echoed in my brain like the ringing of a gong. "Fear nothing! Among such as these do you move every hour of the day and night. Only you and I have seen, for God is merciful and has spared our race from sight. But I am not merciful! I loathe the race which gave these creatures birth—the race which might be so surrounded by invisible, unguessed but blessed beings— and chooses these for its companions! All the world shall see and know. One by one shall they come here, learn the truth, and perish. For who can survive the ultimate of terror? Then I, too, shall find peace, and leave the earth to its heritage of man-created horrors. Do you know what these are—whence they come?"

This voice boomed now like a cathedral bell. I could not answer, him, but he waited for no reply. "Out of the ether— out of the omnipresent ether from whose intangible substance the mind of God made the planets, all living things, and man—man has made these! By his evil thoughts, by his selfish panics, by his lusts and his interminable, never-ending hate he has made them, and they are everywhere! Fear nothing— they cannot harm your body—but let your spirit beware! Fear nothing—but see where there comes to you, its creator, the shape and the body of your FEAR!"

And as he said it I perceived a great Thing coming toward me—a Thing—but consciousness could endure no more. The ringing, threatening voice merged in a roar within my ears, there came a merciful dimming of the terrible, lurid vision, and blank nothingness succeeded upon horror too great for bearing.

IV.

There was a dull, heavy pain above my eyes. I knew that they were closed, that I was dreaming, and that the rack full of colored bottles which I seemed to see so clearly was no more than a part of the dream. There was some vague but imperative reason why I should rouse myself. I wanted to awaken, and thought that by staring very hard indeed I could dissolve this foolish vision of blue and yellow-brown bottles. But instead of dissolving they grew clearer, more solid and substantial of appearance, until suddenly the rest of my senses rushed to the support of sight, and I became aware that my eyes were open, the bottles were quite real, and that I was sitting in a chair, fallen sideways so that my cheek rested most uncomfortably on the table which held the rack.

I straightened up slowly and with difficulty, groping in my dulled brain for some clue to my presence in this unfamiliar place, this laboratory that was lighted only by the rays of an arc light in the street outside its three large windows. Here I sat, alone, and if the aching of cramped limbs meant anything, here I had sat for more than a little time.

Then, with the painful shock which accompanies awakening to the knowledge of some great catastrophe, came memory. It was this very room, shown by the street lamp's rays to be empty of life, which I had seen thronged with creatures too loathsome for description. I staggered to my feet, staring fearfully about. There were the glass-doored cases, the bookshelves, the two tables with their burdens, and the long iron sink above which, now only a dark blotch of shadow, hung the lamp from which had emanated that livid, terrifically revealing illumination. Then the experience had been no dream, but a frightful reality. I was alone here now. With callous indifference my strange host had allowed me to remain for hours unconscious, with not the least effort to aid or revive me. Perhaps, hating me so, he had hoped that I would die there.

At first I made no effort to leave the place. Its appearance filled me with reminiscent loathing. I longed to go, but as yet felt too weak and ill for the effort. Both mentally and physically my condition was deplorable, and for the first time I realized that a shock to the mind may react upon the body as vilely as any debauch of self-indulgence.

Quivering in every nerve and muscle, dizzy with headache and nausea, I dropped back into the chair, hoping that before the old man returned I might recover sufficient self-control to escape him. I knew that he hated me, and why. As I waited, sick, miserable, I understood the man. Shuddering, I recalled the loathsome horrors he had shown me. If the mere desires and emotions of mankind were daily carnified in such forms as those, no wonder that he viewed his fellow beings with detestation and longed only to destroy them.

I thought, too, of the cruel, sensuous faces I had seen in the streets outside—seen for the first time, as if a veil had been withdrawn from eyes hitherto blinded by self-delusion. Fatuously trustful as a month-old puppy, I had lived in a grim, evil world, where goodness is a word and crude selfishness the only actuality. Drearily my thoughts drifted back through my own life, its futile purposes, mistakes and activities. All of evil that I knew returned to overwhelm me. Our gropings toward divinity were a sham, a writhing sunward of slime-covered beasts who claimed sunlight as their heritage, but in their hearts preferred the foul and easy depths.

Even now, though I could neither see nor feel them, this room, the entire world, was acrawl with the beings created by our real natures. I recalled the cringing, contemptible fear to which my spirit had so readily yielded, and the faceless Thing to which the emotion had given birth.

Then abruptly, shockingly, I remembered that every moment I was adding to the horde. Since my mind could conceive only repulsive incubi, and since while I lived I must think, feel, and so continue to shape them, was there no way to check so abominable a succession? My eyes fell on the long shelves with their many-colored bottles. In the chemistry of photography there are deadly poisons—I knew that. Now was the time to end it—now! Let him return and find his desire accomplished. One good thing I could do, if one only. I could abolish my monster-creating self.

V.

My friend Mark Jenkins is an intelligent and usually a very careful man. When he took from "Smiler" Callahan a cigar which had every appearance of being excellent, innocent Havana, the act denoted both intelligence and caution. By very clever work he had traced the poisoning of young Ralph Peeler to Mr. Callahan's door, and he believed this particular cigar to be the mate of one smoked by Peeler just previous to his demise. And if, upon arresting Callahan, he had not confiscated this bit of evidence, it would have doubtless been destroyed by its regrettably unconscientious owner.

But when Jenkins shortly afterward gave me that cigar, as one of his own, he committed one of those almost inconceivable blunders which, I think, are occasionally forced upon clever men to keep them from overweening vanity. Discovering his slight mistake, my detective friend spent the night searching for his unintended victim, myself, and that his search was successful was due to Pietro Marini, a young Italian of Jenkins' acquaintance, whom he met about the hour of 2 a.m. returning from a dance.

Now, Marini had seen me standing on the steps of the house where Doctor Frederick Holt had his laboratory and living rooms, and he had stared at me, not with any ill intent, but because he thought I was the sickest-looking, most ghastly specimen of humanity that he had ever beheld. And, sharing the superstition of his South Street neighbors, he wondered if the worthy doctor had poisoned me as well as Peeler. This suspicion he imparted to Jenkins, who, however, had the best of reasons for believing otherwise. Moreover, as he informed Marini, Holt was dead, having drowned himself late the previous afternoon. An hour or so after our talk in the restaurant news of his suicide reached Jenkins.

It seemed wise to search any place where a very sick-looking young man had been seen to enter, so Jenkins came straight to the laboratory. Across the fronts of those houses was the long sign with its mysterious inscription, "See the Great Unseen," not at all mysterious to the detective. He knew that next door to Doctor Holt's the second floor had been thrown together into a lecture room, where at certain hours a young man employed by settlement workers displayed upon a screen stereopticon views of various deadly bacilli, the germs of diseases appropriate to dirt and indifference. He knew, too, that Doctor Holt himself had helped the educational effort along by providing some really wonderful lantern slides, done by micro-color photography.

On the pavement outside, Jenkins found the two-thirds remnant of a cigar, which he gathered in and came up the steps, a very miserable and self-reproachful detective. Neither outer nor inner door was locked, and in the laboratory he found me, alive, but on the verge of death by another means that he had feared.

In the extreme physical depression following my awakening from drugged sleep, and knowing nothing of its cause, I believed my adventure fact in its entirety. My mentality was at too low an ebb to resist its dreadful suggestion. I was searching among Holt's various bottles when Jenkins burst in. At first I was merely annoyed at the interruption of my purpose, but before the anticlimax of his explanation the mists of obsession drifted away and left me still sick in body, but in spirit happy as any man may well be who has suffered a delusion that the world is wholly bad—and learned that its badness springs from his own poisoned brain.

The malice which I had observed in every face, including young Marini's, existed only in my drug-affected vision. Last week's "popular-science" lecture had been recalled to my sub-conscious mind—the mind that rules dreams and delirium—by the photographic apparatus in Holt's workroom. "See the Great Unseen" assisted materially, and even the corner drug store before which I had paused, with its green-lit show vases, had doubtless played a part. But presently, following some-thing Jenkins told me, I was driven to one protest. "If Holt was not here," I demanded, "if Holt is dead, as you say, how do you account for the fact that I, who have never seen the man, was able to give you an accurate description which you admit to be that of Doctor Frederick Holt?"

He pointed across the room. "See that?" It was a life-size bust portrait, in crayons, the picture of a white-haired man with bushy eyebrows and the most piercing black eyes I had ever seen—until the previous evening. It hung facing the door and near the windows, and the features stood out with a strangely lifelike appearance in the white rays of the arc lamp just out-side. "Upon entering," continued Jenkins, "the first thing you saw was that portrait, and from it your delirium built a living, speaking man. So, there are your white-haired showman, your unnatural fear, your color photography and your pretty green golliwogs all nicely explained for you, Blaisdell, and thank God you're alive to hear the explanation. If you had smoked the whole of that cigar—well, never mind. You didn't. And now, my very dear friend, I think it's high time that you interviewed a real, flesh-and-blood doctor. I'll phone for a taxi."

"Don't," I said. "A walk in the fresh air will do me more good than fifty doctors."

"Fresh air! There's no fresh air on South Street in July," complained Jenkins, but reluctantly yielded.

I had a reason for my preference. I wished to see people, to meet face to face even such stray prowlers as might be about at this hour, nearer sunrise than midnight, and rejoice in the goodness and kindliness of the human countenance—particularly as found in the lower classes.

But even as we were leaving there occurred to me a curious inconsistency.

"Jenkins," I said, "you claim that the reason Holt, when I first met him in the hall, appeared to twice close the door in my face, was because the door never opened until I myself unlatched it."

"Yes," confirmed Jenkins, but he frowned, foreseeing my next question.

"Then why, if it was from that picture that I built so solid, so convincing a vision of the man, did I see Holt in the hall before the door was open?"

"You confuse your memories," retorted Jenkins rather shortly.

"Do I? Holt was dead at that hour, but—*I tell you I saw Holt outside the door!* And what was his reason for committing suicide?"

Before my friend could reply I was across the room, fumbling in the dusk there at the electric lamp above the sink. I got the tin flap open and pulled out the sliding screen, which consisted of two sheets of glass with fabric between, dark on one side, yellow on the other. With it came the very thing I dreaded—a sheet of whitish, parchmentlike, slightly opalescent stuff.

Jenkins was beside me as I held it at arm's length toward the windows. Through it the light of the arc lamp fell—divided into the most astonishingly brilliant rainbow hues. And instead of diminishing the light, it was perceptibly increased in the oddest way. Almost one thought that the sheet itself was luminous, and yet when held in shadow it gave off no light at all.

"Shall we—put it in the lamp again—and try it?" asked Jenkins slowly, and in his voice there was no hint of mockery.

I looked him straight in the eyes. "No," I said, "we won't. I was drugged. Perhaps in that condition I received a merciless revelation of the discovery that caused Holt's suicide, but I don't believe it. Ghost or no ghost, I refuse to ever again believe in the depravity of the human race. If the air and the earth are teeming with invisible horrors, they are *not* of our making, and—the study of demonology is better let alone. Shall we burn this thing, or tear it up?"

"We have no right to do either," returned Jenkins thoughtfully, "but you know, Blaisdell, there's a little too darn much realism about some parts of your 'dream.' I haven't been smoking any doped cigars; but when you held that up to the light, I'll swear I saw—well, never mind. Burn it—send it back to the place it came from."

"South America?" said I.

"A hotter place than that. Burn it."

So he struck a match and we did. It was gone in one great white flash.

A large place was given by the morning papers to the suicide of Doctor Frederick Holt, caused, it was surmised, by mental derangement brought about by his unjust implication in the Peeler murder. It seemed an inadequate reason, since he had never been arrested, but no other was ever discovered.

Of course, our action in destroying that "membrane" was illegal and rather precipitate, but, though he won't talk about it, I know that Jenkins agrees with me—doubt is sometimes better than certainty, and there are marvels better left unproved. Those, for instance, which concern the Powers of Evil.

In the year 1920

3 Jan. Russian Civil War: The Red Army recaptures Tsaritsyn (Volgograd) from the White Army.

10 Jan. The League of Nations is established.

17 Jan. Prohibition begins in the USA, one year after the 18th Amendment was ratified by the states.

23 Jan. The Netherlands refuses demands by the Allies to extradite Wilhelm II.

2 Feb. The Tartu Peace Treaty is signed, ending the Estonian War of Independence.

24 Feb. Adolf Hitler presents his National Socialist Program to the National Socialist German Workers' Party in Munich.

23 April The Grand National Assembly of Turkey is founded by Mustafa Kemal Atatürk.

14 Aug. The 1920 Summer Olympics open in Antwerp, Belgium.

18 Aug. The 19th Amendment is ratified, guaranteeing women's suffrage in the USA.

4 Sept. Mahatma Gandhi launches the Non-Cooperation Movement in India.

16 Sept. Wall Street bombing: a bomb explodes in front of the J. P. Morgan Building in New York City, killing 40 people.

2 Nov. Warren G. Harding defeats James M. Cox to win the US Presidential Election.

11 Nov. State funeral of the Unknown Warrior at Westminster Abbey, London.

21 Nov. Bloody Sunday: the IRA shoot the Cairo gang; the Auxiliary Division of the Royal Irish Constabulary open fire on a crowd at a Gaelic Athletic Association football match.

The Cats of Ulthar

H.P. Lovecraft

It is said that in Ulthar, which lies beyond the river Skai, no man may kill a cat; and this I can verily believe as I gaze upon him who sitteth purring before the fire. For the cat is cryptic, and close to strange things which men cannot see. He is the soul of antique Aegyptus, and bearer of tales from forgotten cities in Meroë and Ophir. He is the kin of the jungle's lords, and heir to the secrets of hoary and sinister Africa. The Sphinx is his cousin, and he speaks her language; but he is more ancient than the Sphinx, and remembers that which she hath forgotten.

In Ulthar, before ever the burgesses forbade the killing of cats, there dwelt an old cotter and his wife who delighted to trap and slay the cats of their neighbours. Why they did this I know not; save that many hate the voice of the cat in the night, and take it ill that cats should run stealthily about yards and gardens at twilight. But whatever the reason, this old man and woman took pleasure in trapping and slaying every cat which came near to their hovel; and from some of the sounds heard after dark, many villagers fancied that the manner of slaying was exceedingly peculiar. But the villagers did not discuss such things with the old man and his wife; because of the habitual expression on the withered faces of the two, and because their cottage was so small and so darkly hidden under spreading oaks at the back of a neglected yard. In truth, much as the owners of cats hated these odd folk, they feared them more; and instead of berating them as brutal assassins, merely took care that no cherished pet or mouser should stray toward the remote hovel under the dark trees. When through some unavoidable oversight a cat was missed, and sounds heard after dark, the loser would lament impotently; or console himself by thanking Fate that it was not one of his children who had thus vanished. For the people of Ulthar were simple, and knew not whence it is all cats first came.

One day a caravan of strange wanderers from the South entered the narrow cobbled streets of Ulthar. Dark wanderers they were, and unlike the other roving folk who passed through the village twice every year. In the market-place they told fortunes for silver, and bought gay beads from the merchants. What was the land of these wanderers none could tell; but it was seen that they were given to strange prayers, and that they had painted on the sides of their wagons strange figures with human bodies and the heads of cats, hawks, rams, and lions. And the leader of the caravan wore a head-dress with two horns and a curious disc betwixt the horns.

There was in this singular caravan a little boy with no father or mother, but only a tiny black kitten to cherish. The plague had not been kind to him, yet had left him this small furry thing to mitigate his sorrow; and when one is very young, one can find great relief in the lively antics of a black kitten. So the boy whom the dark people called Menes smiled more often than he wept as he sate playing with his graceful kitten on the steps of an oddly painted wagon.

On the third morning of the wanderers' stay in Ulthar, Menes could not find his kitten; and as he sobbed aloud in the market-place certain villagers told him of the old man and his wife, and of sounds heard in the night. And when he heard these things his sobbing gave place to meditation, and finally to prayer. He stretched out his arms toward the sun and prayed in a tongue no villager could understand; though indeed the villagers did not try very hard to understand, since their attention was mostly taken up by the sky and the odd shapes the clouds were assuming. It was very peculiar, but as the little boy uttered his petition there seemed to form overhead the shadowy, nebulous figures of exotic things; of hybrid creatures crowned with horn-flanked discs. Nature is full of such illusions to impress the imaginative.

That night the wanderers left Ulthar, and were never seen again. And the householders were troubled when they noticed that in all the village there was not a cat to be found. From each hearth the familiar cat had vanished; cats large and small, black, grey, striped, yellow, and white. Old Kranon, the burgomaster, swore that the dark folk had taken the cats away in revenge for the killing of Menes' kitten; and cursed the caravan and the little boy. But Nith, the lean notary, declared that the old cotter and his wife were more likely persons to suspect; for their hatred of cats was notorious and increasingly bold. Still, no one durst complain to the sinister couple; even when little Atal, the innkeeper's son, vowed that he had at twilight seen all the cats of Ulthar in that accursed yard under the trees, pacing very slowly and solemnly in a circle around the cottage, two abreast, as if in performance of some unheard-of rite of beasts. The villagers did not know how much to believe from so small a boy; and though they feared that the evil pair had charmed the cats to their death, they preferred not to chide the old cotter till they met him outside his dark and repellent yard.

So Ulthar went to sleep in vain anger; and when the people awaked at dawn—behold! every cat was back at his accustomed hearth! Large and small, black, grey, striped, yellow, and white, none was missing. Very sleek and fat did the cats appear, and sonorous with purring content. The citizens talked with one another of the affair, and marvelled not a little. Old Kranon again insisted that it was the dark folk who had taken them, since cats did not return alive from the cottage of the ancient man and his wife. But all agreed on one thing: that the refusal of all the cats to eat their portions of meat or drink their saucers of milk was exceedingly curious. And for two whole days the sleek, lazy cats of Ulthar would touch no food, but only doze by the fire or in the sun.

It was fully a week before the villagers noticed that no lights were appearing at dusk in the windows of the cottage under the trees. Then the lean Nith remarked that no one had seen the old man or his wife since the night the cats were away. In another week the burgomaster decided to overcome his fears and call at the strangely silent dwelling as a matter of duty, though in so doing he was careful to take with him Shang the blacksmith and Thul the cutter of stone as witnesses. And when they had broken down the frail door they found only this: two cleanly picked human skeletons on the earthen floor, and a number of singular beetles crawling in the shadowy corners.

There was subsequently much talk among the burgesses of Ulthar. Zath, the coroner, disputed at length with Nith, the lean notary; and Kranon and Shang and Thul were overwhelmed with questions. Even little Atal, the innkeeper's son, was closely questioned and given a sweetmeat as reward. They talked of the old cotter and his wife, of the caravan of dark wanderers, of small Menes and his black kitten, of the prayer of Menes and of the sky during that prayer, of the doings of the cats on the night the caravan left, and of what was later found in the cottage under the dark trees in the repellent yard.

And in the end the burgesses passed that remarkable law which is told of by traders in Hatheg and discussed by travellers in Nir; namely, that in Ulthar no man may kill a cat.

...He had at twilight seen all the cats of Ulthar in that accursed yard under the trees, pacing very slowly and solemnly in a circle around the cottage, two abreast, as if in performance of some unheard-of rite of beasts.

Redcap Manor

A.L. Randolph

Until it was demolished in 1949, Redcap Manor was considered one of the most haunted places in England. Although little remembered today, the once renowned Edwardian ghost-and-fairy-hunter Arthur L. Randolph conducted a series of experiments with electromagnetic fields in the manor in the early 20th century, with his reported sightings of boggarts, barghests, banshees, and bloodsuckers causing a considerable stir in society at the time.

The long-lost notes of A.L. Randolph were recently rediscovered and are published here for the first time. Randolph's haunting recollections of faeries and phantoms, accompanied by evocative artwork by Rustan Curman, shine an electric light on Britain's hidden world. Enter Redcap Manor, if you dare…